DAWN LEE MCKENNA'S

OVERBOARD

A *FORGOTTEN COAST* SUSPENSE NOVEL:
BOOK TEN

2018

A SWEET TEA PRESS PUBLICATION

First published in the United States by Sweet Tea Press

©2018 Dawn Lee McKenna. All rights reserved.

Edited by Debbie Maxwell Allen

Cover by Shayne Rutherford
wickedgoodbookcovers.com

Interior Design by Colleen Sheehan
ampersandbookinteriors.com

for

Kirk and Faith

family

SPECIAL
ACKNOWLEDGMENTS

There are a lot of real people who appear in my books from time to time, many of them becoming readers' favorite secondary characters. There are also a lot of people who help me to write in more detail than I otherwise could, or to write about things that I really don't know much about.

I owe a great deal to Captain Skip Shiver, former Sheriff, and current charter captain, who has spent years with the volunteer search and rescue team in Franklin County. Thanks to Skip, I was able to put Maggie where I needed her, when I needed her to be there. His knowledge of the tides, currents, navigational aids and other elements of the Gulf near Apalach was absolutely indispensable. Those of you familiar with the waters in the area might notice that I have played with the locations of some of the buoys and towers in the Gulf. This wasn't because of bad information from Skip; I just needed the Gulf to cooperate with my story.

Special thanks, as always, go out to John Solomon, formerly with the Franklin County Sheriff's Office and now Executive Director of the Apalachicola Bay Area Chamber of Commerce. He has been indispensable since the first chapter of the first book in this series. I'm grateful to have had him as a technical advisor; I'm even more grateful to have become his friend.

There are several other residents of Apalachicola who have become characters in this series, including Kirk Lynch of Apalachicola Chocolate & Coffee, and Linda Joseph from the Water Street Hotel & Marina. Thank you, you guys, for letting me take liberties with you.

CHAPTER
ONE

Maggie tried to make her terrified brain change focus. She couldn't think about the fact that she was treading water miles from shore, in seventy feet of water, in the Gulf. The Gulf that she used to love so much before her phobia of sharks drove her from it.

She had to get away. She needed to get away from the chum. She needed to get away from the body. She needed to do that now.

"Ah!" she screamed out, then ducked underwater.

She forced herself down several feet, below the reach of the deck lights. She needed to get over to the port side. For the first few moments, they would be focusing on the starboard side. The hull was just a darker shape in dark water, but she could make it out. She felt her left contact lens become dislodged. She blinked twice and it was gone.

She figured the beam, or width, of the boat was about twelve or thirteen feet, and she was about seven feet away when she went under. Ordinarily, twenty feet was nothing. When she was younger, she could very easily swim three times as far underwater. But she hadn't been underwater in a long time, and she was scared, and she was wearing boots.

She swam beneath the boat, praying her natural buoyancy wouldn't lift her. She was only about five feet beneath it. She swam using a careful breaststroke, trying to override her fear in order to stroke as efficiently and effectively as possible. If buoyancy took over, she'd bump against the hull and they'd wait for a chance to shoot her. If she ran out of breath and panicked, bumping against the hull, they'd wait for a chance to shoot her, or she'd just drown. If they decided to leave now, they'd probably run her over.

At the forefront of her mind, though, was the fact that a bloody body and several bloody chunks of fish were just a few yards behind her. The thought made her want to thrash, to scream, to pop to the surface and scramble up the port side of the boat to be shot. The sharks would still get her, but maybe she wouldn't know.

Instead, she forced her strong legs to frog kick in spite of the boots, forced herself to dive a foot or so deeper despite her need for air. Once she cleared the hull, she fought the instinct to surface immediately. She swam a good ten feet farther, as far as she could manage on the air she had. It was only about three feet past the pool of light cast by the boat, but it would have to do. Then her task became dropping her feet and easing her body to the surface, instead of scrambling for it.

Her chest felt like someone was holding a heavy, heated weight against it, and her temples pounded, but she stroked gently, and when her head broke the surface she gulped the clean, cool air as silently as she could.

From her position, with only her head above water, she couldn't see the men on the boat, but she could see a flashlight strafing the water astern of the boat, then swinging back toward the starboard side. She couldn't make out what anyone was saying, but more than one man was speaking.

Suddenly, one of the men cursed loudly, and there was a whooshing sound on the other side of the boat.

"Did you *see* that?" one of the voices yelled.

Complete and total terror enveloped Maggie. She knew what he saw. She knew what she'd heard. A shark or sharks had found the chum, or the body, or both.

Her breathing became shallow and unhelpful. Her face tingled around the edges and every follicle above water expanded. In just a few seconds, her limbs started to feel numb, though she was still treading water.

Away.

She needed to be away, more than she needed to give vent to her abject terror. The idea of putting her face back in the water was almost paralyzing, even though she'd known before that the sharks would be there, *were* there. But now she knew how close they were, and she knew that more were coming.

The shark who'd caused such excitement had actually done her a favor, by making it seem more likely that she'd been pulled under. Even so, the men still might move to the port side to search for her. She needed to not be on the surface until she was out of range of their flashlights, at least. But which way?

She looked up at the sky, but the clouds were low and thick. There was no moon, and there were no stars. The lack of moon might work in her favor at the moment but would be a hindrance later. If there was a later.

Get your act together, Maggie. Think. Why are you looking for celestial bodies? Go back the way you came.

She took a long, silent breath, blew it out just as quietly, and dove.

CHAPTER
TWO

It was comin' up a storm, as her grandfather used to say.

Maggie Hamilton leaned against the rail on the back deck, her coffee mug warm in her hands. A brisk breeze was coming in off the bay just beyond the back yard. It was still too dark to see the water, but Maggie could smell the brine and mud. She could just taste a hint of metal in the air, and that, coupled with the breeze and the humidity, told her most of what she needed to know about that day's forecast. She'd know the rest once it was light enough to see the clouds.

Despite the inhumane heat and humidity, summer was Maggie's favorite season. It was the season of true storms, not just a daily ten-minute rain at 3:15

in the afternoon. Summer, particularly mid-July, as it was now, was the season of tropical depressions and low-pressure systems, lightning that blinded, thunder that made the arteries vibrate, and great, pounding rains. Maggie loved them all.

Raised as the daughter of an oysterman and having loved to help Daddy out on the oyster beds, she'd learned early in life to read the sky and the water. She'd spent most of her growing-up either on the Gulf or in it; had considered it her natural habitat until she'd developed a debilitating fear of sharks. It wasn't the sharks' fault, it wasn't even the Gulf's. It was just an unfortunate side-effect of PTSD. The PTSD rarely troubled Maggie anymore, but the water was still lost to her. She was on it every chance she got, but she was never in it.

She sometimes grieved, the way she might over the loss of a friend.

She drained her cup, then went back into the kitchen through the sliding-glass door. She nearly tripped over her rooster, Stoopid, who'd been waiting, beak to glass, for her to come back inside.

"Out of the way, Stoopid," Maggie hissed, glad her cup had been empty. She walked over to the counter and pulled another mug from a shelf as Stoopid, wings flapping and diaper rustling, landed on the glazed barnwood counter.

Maggie grabbed the coffee pot, and poured herself a refill, then added a little milk and one spoon of sugar. Stoopid peered into her cup the whole time, like a chemical engineer analyzing the coffee's make-up. He let out a stream of chirrups, warbles and hiccups.

"I already know how I take my coffee," Maggie said drily. He continued his commentary as she poured the second cup and added milk and two sugars. "I know how he takes his coffee, too," she added.

"Crap, you're not giving him his own coffee now, are you?" Wyatt asked as he walked in from the living room.

"No, this is yours," Maggie answered.

Stoopid let out an asthmatic crow as Wyatt reached the counter.

"Look at me," Wyatt said to him. "I *am* up."

He kissed his wife on the forehead, then took a grateful drink of his coffee. "You need to watch him. I'm pretty sure he was nipping at my coffee yesterday. He was running around the kitchen like a spider on speed."

"I told you to take it with you when you shave," Maggie said distractedly, looking out the window over the sink. "I've gotta run, but it's getting ready storm. Can you drop Kyle off at Mom and Daddy's?"

Kyle was her twelve-year-old son, soon to be thir-teen, and the image of his late father, David.

"Yeah. What's he doing over there?"

"He and Daddy are going to get started on that sewing table for Mom."

Maggie drank as much as she could of her second cup, then set it down in the sink and got up on tiptoe for another kiss. Maggie was five-three and her husband was six-four. Physically, they were oppo-sites. In personality, they were at right angles, but somehow, it worked for them. Wyatt wrapped an arm around Maggie and gave her a long kiss as Stoopid suggested improvements to his technique.

"Take him with you," Wyatt said.

Maggie smiled at him as she grabbed her keys, badge and service weapon from a basket on the counter. "Would you leave a note for Sky?" she asked, meaning her seventeen-year-old daughter. "Tell her to let The Girls out into the chicken run if the storms pass."

"You're thinking she'll be awake at some point today?" Wyatt asked, but there was no sarcasm to it. Sky had just graduated high school after busting her butt to earn a 4.2 average. In a month and a half, she'd start busting her butt at Florida State. Nobody begrudged her a few weeks of lounging.

"She's doing something with Bella this afternoon," Maggie said. "She'll be up eventually. What are you doing today?"

"Oh, exciting things," Wyatt answered wryly. "This morning, I'm meeting with the county commissioners to update them on our crime and arrest rates. Then late this afternoon I'm meeting with John Solomon and local news directors to talk about responsibility in journalism or some kind of crap."

Several months ago, Wyatt had resigned his position as Sheriff so that he and Maggie could marry. Now, he was the Public Liaison Officer for the Franklin County Sheriff's Office. Every now and then, he still got to get out on the front lines, if the case was big enough or they were short-staffed. Maggie worried that he missed being a "real" cop, but he assured her that he was just biding time for two years, until he took early retirement at fifty, and that he was quite happy with his decision, unless she was being what he called an 'asspain.'

"Why isn't Bledsoe doing that?" Curtis Bledsoe was the sheriff Governor Troy Spaulding had appointed to replace Wyatt.

"He said he's got an appointment with his accountant in Tallahassee at six-thirty. Why don't we need an accountant?"

"Because we know how to use a calculator. Are you gonna be done in time for dinner? We're having Dwight and Amy over, remember?"

"Crap, I forgot!" Wyatt drained his coffee. "I'm supposed to pick up the cake."

"I'll get the cake," Maggie said. "But you'll be here, right? It's important."

Maggie's partner, Dwight Shultz, had been shot the previous month, by a kid who hadn't really intended to shoot anyone; he'd just been scared. Ryan was now awaiting trial, Dwight was getting around better every day with the help of a cane, and since his release from the hospital a couple of weeks ago, he'd been visiting Ryan at Franklin Correctional. Tomorrow would be Dwight's first day back at work; a half-day, at his desk, but he would be back nonetheless.

"Yeah, no problem," Wyatt answered. "If they run long, I'll use it as an out. Seven o'clock, right?"

"Yep. Lasagna." Maggie walked to the sliding door.

"You're at your most appealing when you're making lasagna," Wyatt said, winking at her.

She tried winking back, but mainly succeeded in looking like one of her contacts had rolled up into her eye socket. She opened the door. "I'm gonna feed The Girls on my way out."

"Hey," he snapped. She stopped. "You love me."

"I do love you."

"I love you, too," Wyatt said. "As evidenced by my ability to remember to say it."

"Jerk," she responded, as she stepped out onto the deck.

⚓   ⚓   ⚓

It did storm, periodically, all day. There wasn't much wind to it, no more than 10-15 knots, but Maggie delighted in the prodigious rainfall.

The majority of it was gone by late afternoon, though the forecast, and the barometer, said more would be forthcoming. By six, the sky was low and steely gray, the humidity startling. There were no parking spaces in front of Apalachicola Coffee on Market Street, so she went around the corner and down the block on Commerce and parked in the empty lot across from the Chamber of Commerce.

As she got out of her Cherokee, she glanced over at the Chamber to see if John's truck was there. John Solomon had been a good friend for years; they'd worked together at the Sheriff's Office until he'd taken his twenty and taken over as director of the Chamber. Just last month, he'd been elected Mayor, a job for which he was almost supernaturally suited. Van Johnson, Sr. had been mayor for more years than

Maggie could count, and everyone was devoted to him, but he'd chosen not to run for another term.

John's truck wasn't in the lot and wasn't parked on the street in front of the Chamber, either, and Maggie remembered the meeting with Wyatt and the news people. She walked around the corner to Market Street and into Apalachicola Coffee. Despite the fact that July was a busy tourist month, the shop was fairly quiet, due to the hour. Too early for after-dinner coffee, too late for lunch. Earlier in the day and after dinner, the brick-walled, tin-ceilinged shop was always hopping.

Normally, Maggie wouldn't have one of her three-shot lattes at six o'clock, unless she was working late, but she was there. The aroma of roasting beans caressed her like a loving mother, and Kirk's new espresso machine, The Excessively Sexy Machine, was right there on the back counter, doing nothing. She made a beeline for it.

One of Kirk's part-time employees, a blue-haired man in his late seventies, was wiping the glass candy counter with a languid thoroughness. He didn't look up as Maggie walked in. Another employee, Mona, was helping some customers at the gelato counter, and she smiled as Maggie walked past.

She had been at the counter for a minute or two when Mona called out, "Spaz! Tell Kirk that Maggie's here for the cake."

Spaz stopped wiping and looked around slowly like a turtle, until his eyes settled on Maggie. He licked his lips and coughed, put down the rag, and started making his way toward the kitchen in back, at a pace that would have allowed a one-legged gator to overtake him.

He was almost to the short hall that led to the back when Kirk Lynch met him halfway, carrying a white cake box. "Forget it," he muttered to Spaz as he passed him.

Spaz looked around, blinked a few times, then continued on to the kitchen. Kirk put the cake box down on the counter in front of Maggie and lifted the lid. It was a beautiful, dense-looking dark chocolate cake, with a pretty good approximation of an SO badge painted in thin frosting.

"That looks great," Maggie said.

"It should. It took me half the day," Kirk replied. His sandy hair, going gray in places, was tied up in a ponytail. A burnt-orange bandana covered his head. His t-shirt declared him the guardian of the caffeine galaxy. "Is this it?"

Maggie chewed at the corner of her lip and glanced over at The Exceptionally Sexy.

"It's 6:00, not 2:45," Kirk said.

"But I'm here," she replied.

"You were here at 2:45, too," he said flatly.

"What, are you in the business of *not* selling coffee?" she asked testily. There was no such thing as a simple transaction with Kirk; every visit seemed to necessitate either a defensive stance or a little pleading.

"I'm in the business of not giving my customers heart attacks," he replied, unfazed.

"I didn't get to drink my 2:45."

"I'm sure that happens," he replied drily. "Not ever, not once."

"Are you saying I can't have any coffee?" Maggie asked, incredulous. This was a coffee place. Selling coffee was its reason for existence. The chocolate and gelato and pastries were irrelevant.

Kirk reached over to a regular coffee pot, grabbed a to-go cup and filled it halfway with coffee. Then he replaced the pot and pushed the cup toward Maggie. She peered down into it, then looked back up at him.

"This is regular coffee."

"This is the best *regular* coffee in the Panhandle."

"But I drink espresso," Maggie said, trying not to hiss.

"And if you come in in the morning, or at 2:45, or even both, that's what I'll give you," Kirk said. "Three shots, no foam, no cardboard, not too hot. Because you're a super-tough law enforcement officer but you have a delicate tongue, unless it's moving."

"It's half a cup."

"It's also on the house."

"So, you're giving me something I don't want, but giving it to me for free?"

"Well, I'm not a complete jerk."

THREE

WEDNESDAY, JULY 11TH 6:10 PM

A few minutes later, her half-cup of undesirable coffee in one hand and her cake in the other, Maggie walked back to her car. She noticed that the lights were still on in the flower shop next to the gravel lot. She put her coffee in the cupholder and the cake on the passenger seat. Her cell phone was plugged into the charger, and she picked it up to check the time. The screen was still dark. She jiggled the charger out and then back into the port. She was pretty sure her charger was finally kaput. She glanced at her old Timex. 6:10.

She'd made the lasagna the night before, and Sky had called just before five to assure her mother that she would put it in the oven at six sharp. It was a five-minute drive home, so Maggie had a little time.

She grabbed her wallet and shut the door and went into the flower shop to get something pretty and simple for the kitchen table. It was a special occasion, after all.

The Blooming Idiot was in a cute little brick building, with blue trim around the windows. Like most of the buildings downtown, it dated at least back to the turn of the century. William and Robert had done a nice job of creating a bright little space that was fresh without being too trendy. William, a slight, unnaturally blond man in his mid-fifties, was at the back counter when Maggie walked in. He looked up from some mail as the bell over the door tinkled.

"Robert," William called. "The little sheriff is here!"

Maggie tried not to roll her eyes. Robert, a much taller and broader man with slicked-back dark hair, appeared from the back as Maggie made her way to the counter. "Oh, hello," he said cautiously.

"What's happened?" William demanded, somehow managing to give the impression that he was simultaneously pursing his lips.

"I'm having company," Maggie answered.

"What does that mean?"

"It means I want something pretty for the table. Nobody's dead."

"Oh. Well, good," William said. "It's been a nice summer season so far."

"Very smooth," Robert elaborated.

"We haven't had to put up with a dead guy since… what?" William looked at Robert.

"March," Robert supplied. "But that was a woman."

"Nevertheless," William said, waving him off. "We'd appreciate it if no one died until after the Seafood Festival."

"By violent means," Robert expounded. "Death of old age or disease is good for business."

"I'll see what I can do," Maggie said quietly. "In the meantime, could I have some of those hydrangeas?"

"Hm." William looked over at the pink hydrangeas, then back at Maggie. "A little pedestrian, don't you think?"

"Uninspired," Robert elaborated.

"It's just dinner in the kitchen with some close friends," Maggie said. "And I need to be home by seven."

William waved away her concerns. "We are professionally trained, certified florists, and members in good standing of the Florida State Florists Association, the American Institute of Floral Designers, and the Society of American Florists."

"Okay." Maggie had no idea why this was relevant.

"The Society of Southern Florists, as well," Robert said helpfully.

"They don't count," William said. "We don't go to their functions anymore."

Robert looked at Maggie. "A hundred and thirty-five dollars for frozen cordon bleu and demonstrations of arrangements we stopped doing decades ago."

"Baby's breath everywhere," William announced, flinging an arm.

"It was like K-Tel Records presents the Top Floral Hits of the 80s," Robert added.

"All of this is to say that we don't need an hour to put something together for a casual dinner," William said.

"Great," Maggie replied. "Whatever you think is best, then."

"The deep purple larkspur, naturally," William said.

"In our opinion," Robert clarified.

⚓ ⚓ ⚓

The only thing Wyatt hated more than meetings with officials, reporters, bosses, or anybody really, was chickpeas. He hated chickpeas more. And sea cucumbers, he hated those more, too, for different reasons.

He was only awake and pretending to be engaged because of John Solomon. He and John were good friends, and John's love for Franklin County, where he'd been born and raised, was as genuine as it got.

For these reasons, Wyatt was trying really hard to show some respect, but he didn't want to be there. They could talk to the news people all they wanted about responsible reporting, but the news people didn't care. The news people could assure them from here to next week that they'd be responsible, but nobody else in the room believed them, so what was the point?

Wyatt had done his schtick and he was just waiting for John to wrap everything up. The news director from WCND was whining about transparency and Wyatt was trying not to reach across the table and slap him, so he pulled his phone out and shot Maggie a text. Texting was new to him, and he hated it almost as much as he hated sea cucumbers, so it took him a minute.

If I don't make it home, it's because I got bored to death. My insurance papers are in the left-hand drawer of my desk.

He looked back up, put on his paying attention face, and waited a moment before looking back down at his phone. Maggie hadn't replied. The thingy didn't say his text had been read, either. It didn't even say the text had been delivered. He hated the thingy, too.

He was notoriously laid-back and generally of good humor, but he was tired, his pseudo-cop duties were irritating him, and he wanted a shower and a Mountain Dew. He also wanted to be beltless and shoeless.

There was a wave of rustling and shuffling that mercifully alerted Wyatt to the fact that the meeting was over. He stood up with everyone else and watched as John thanked and shook and politicked. Wyatt nodded goodbye at the various news people, and then John caught his eye.

"Hey man, stick around for a minute, okay?" he asked.

"Sure," Wyatt said.

Once the last journalist had left, John reached over and shut the conference room door, and he and Wyatt sat back down.

"You got a few minutes?" John asked him, his face typically, and naturally, open and friendly. He was in his early forties, slightly stocky, with sun-bleached blond hair that was headed somewhere else.

"No, John, I left already," Wyatt said.

"Don't be a jerk," John said, laughing.

"Your vending machine is out of Mountain Dew, and I was trapped in here with those people for over an hour."

"Well, not because I don't like you," John said, smiling. "Listen, I know I should tell Maggie first, but she's not here, plus I tried calling her right before we got started and her phone's dead."

"How do you know her phone's dead?"

John gave him a blank look. "'Cause she never turns it off on purpose, but it went straight to voice-mail."

"Ah." Wyatt frowned at his phone's screen. He'd proudly carried a flip phone until he and Maggie got married, then reluctantly got an iPhone so they could all be on the same plan. "Is that why she hasn't answered my text?"

"Let me see it," John said, holding out his hand. Wyatt handed it to him. "Yeah, see,? It hasn't been delivered. Maybe she lost her charger."

"Maybe," Wyatt answered. "So, what's up? What's this about Maggie?"

"You can't say anything to anybody but her, man, because it's not been formally announced yet."

"What hasn't?"

"Dan Bernhard's retiring."

Dan was the Chief of the Apalachicola PD and had been for fifteen years.

"Retiring? Why?"

"What do you mean, why? Because he can. He's gonna open up a fishing charter business. It's his life's dream."

"Huh." Wyatt nodded. "Okay. So?"

"So, I want to ask Maggie if she'll take the job."

Wyatt tried not to gape. He was more or less unsuccessful. Maggie's grandfather had been the Chief of Police up until sometime in the seventies, but there were six whole people on the PD staff, and that included the chief.

"You want Maggie to move from the SO to PD," Wyatt said. It wasn't a question.

"Yeah. I mean, that's mine and the city council's call," John said. "You know, to offer it."

"But she's with the SO," Wyatt said pointlessly. "Why not Lon Woodman?"

Lon was the most senior officer with PD, and an excellent cop.

"He don't want it," John said. "Says it's too much hassle."

Wyatt stared at him for a minute. This was completely unexpected. His first instinct was that Maggie was devoted to the SO, and had worked her butt off to achieve her rank. She was also one of only two lieutenants in the Criminal Investigation Unit, at least until Dwight stopped gimping around and got back to work.

"Everybody else over there's too green," John added, like Wyatt was the one he needed to convince. "I'd ask you, but you got less than two years till you can take your pension, and I know that's what you're planning on doing."

Wyatt nodded. "Yeah, that's about the size of it," he agreed. "Listen, I honestly don't know what Maggie will think about it. She has a tendency to surprise me."

"She's been that way since third grade, man." John and Maggie had gone to school together. So had everybody else around the age of forty.

Wyatt stood, and John stood with him. Wyatt shrugged. "Talk to her. That's all I can tell you."

"If she considers it, what's your opinion gonna be?"

"My opinion is that she can do whatever she wants," Wyatt said. "But I don't mind one bit if she spends her days writing parking tickets and consoling burgled tourists. I'm a little put out with her getting shot at."

WEDNESDAY, JULY 11TH 6:3 2PM

Maggie got into the car, laid the paper-wrapped flowers down on top of the cake box and put the keys in the ignition. She rolled the windows down to let some of the heat escape and made a spur-of-the-moment decision to take a quick walk over to Riverfront Park.

It was just around the corner, but the empty lot behind the parking lot made a shortcut. She rolled the passenger window down and tucked her small purse underneath her front seat. Then she pocketed her keys, grabbed her coffee, and got back out. She didn't bother pulling her cell phone from the charger. She'd just be a minute, and theft wasn't exactly epidemic in downtown Apalach.

She walked through the weedy lot, coming out onto Water Street just catty-corner from Riverfront Park.

Riverfront was small, but an important part of downtown Apalach. There were a few spots for day docking, and usually, one or two of them were taken by the beautiful old shrimp boats that Maggie loved so much. There was a grassy area between the street and the dock, with a few benches and a nice fountain. Except for during holidays and other events, it was a quiet and restful spot.

Just over a year ago, during the Independence Day celebration, Maggie had watched as her ex-husband, David, her best friend since fifth grade, had been killed by an explosion on his shrimp boat. Murdered. It had taken almost a year for her to be able to come back to this spot that she'd always loved so much.

She walked over to the seawall that separated the southern end of the park from the house next to it. It was here that she'd waved to David as he'd headed out for a night of shrimping. It was here that she'd watched him wave back, his almost-black hair glinting in the last of the sunlight, his smile wide and content.

Even though they'd been divorced for almost six years, he'd still been the best friend she'd ever had.

Maggie watched the current as it gently disturbed the surface of Scipio Creek. The bridge that led from Apalachicola to Eastpoint curved upward just down the creek, and beyond it was the beautiful Apalachicola Bay, the life's blood of Franklin County. Generations of shrimpers, fishermen, and oystermen had farmed the greenish-blue bay the way generations of men in the Midwest had farmed the black dirt. It was everything.

Maggie turned away from the water and walked over to one of the black wrought iron benches, not quite ready to be done…what? Paying her respects? Acknowledging, with gratitude, that the pain was no longer so profound?

She had just sat down when she heard a car on the street behind her, and looked over her shoulder automatically, without any real interest. She was surprised to see that it was her boss, Sheriff Curtis Bledsoe, at the wheel of his Chrysler Something Fancy that she could never remember. She looked at her watch. It was just after 6:30, and she needed to go, but if Bledsoe had an appointment in Tallahassee at six-thirty, he wouldn't be on Water Street at just before seven.

She wasn't particularly suspicious, and only marginally interested, but her interest piqued when she walked back to the street and saw his car had pulled into the gravel area at the day docks just a block or so past Sea-Fair Seafood Wholesalers. That, she did find curious, since she knew Bledsoe didn't own a boat.

She considered her lack of time for a moment, then headed that way, her hiking boots crunching in the gravel and broken oyster shells that lined the street. She couldn't see Bledsoe's car; he'd pulled it pretty close to the dock, and there was a small, white storage building in her way. As she approached the storage building, she heard the unmistakable sound of twin diesels, one of her favorite sounds in the world.

Sure enough, once she rounded the storage building, she saw the stern and cockpit of a sportfisher. She didn't have a chance to try to see what kind; Bledsoe was just closing his car door and looked up at her with surprise clear in his eyes. A slight man, with slightly receding blond hair, he was almost uniformly nondescript.

"Lieutenant," he said hesitantly.

"Sheriff," she replied, stopping near his rear bumper. She didn't dislike him as much as she used to, but she didn't like him so much that she was above messing with him a little. "How was the accountant?"

He gave her a quick smile as he walked toward her. "Oh, I had to reschedule," he said. "Friends in town."

Maggie glanced over her shoulder at the boat, then turned back to Bledsoe. He looked odd, dressed as he was in Bermuda shorts and a polo shirt.

"There's still some snotty weather coming." She took a sip of her coffee.

"Yeah, but they really want to do some fishing," Bledsoe said, trying for a grin.

Maggie looked down at his loafers, and she saw him see her do it. He'd dressed down, yes, but he wasn't really dressed for fishing. The first thought that occurred to Maggie was that he was heading out with a woman he shouldn't be heading out with. He was single, but if he was messing with a married woman, that would be frowned upon in this small community.

It was none of her business, and she no longer felt like playing with him. She was about to tell him to have fun or be careful or whatever, and get herself on home, when she heard the crunching of gravel behind her.

She turned to see two men she didn't know. They both looked to be in their thirties, and both were fit and fairly large. The one with dark brown hair stayed a couple of steps behind the one who was losing a great deal of his blond hair prematurely. They were both wearing cargo shorts and casual, short-sleeved button-down shirts, but they didn't look at home in them. At least they'd worn deck shoes. The blond man's eyes met Maggie's for just a moment, then he smiled past her.

"Curt, you brought a guest," he said pleasantly.

Bledsoe, behind her, didn't reply, and the man turned his gaze back to Maggie as he held out a hand. "Hello. I'm Curt's cousin, Noel."

Maggie shook his hand briefly. She didn't like him. Her gut told her she had reason not to. "Maggie Hamilton," she said politely, then withdrew her hand.

"Very nice to meet you. And you're a friend of Curt's?"

"We work together," she answered.

He glanced over her shoulder at Bledsoe. Maggie would have looked, too, but she wasn't ready to turn her back on the strangers.

"I can't imagine having to work for this guy," Noel said, his smile dimming just a bit.

Maggie was about to say something noncommittal and leave when something hit her between the shoulder blades and every inch of her body seized up. She heard the crackling of the electrical current, but it seemed to come from a distance. Every muscle in her body had a Charlie horse, all at once, and she cried out.

It was the longest five seconds of her life, and just as the current let go of her, and she let go of her coffee, she heard a pop, and two more probes hit her back. She felt her legs give way, sensed that she was falling to her knees. The man named Noel helped her out with a right hook to her left temple, and then there was just nothing.

⚓ ⚓ ⚓

Bennett Boudreaux leaned back in his leather desk chair and stared out the window at the deepening gloom.

There were no buildings taller than three stories in Apalach, and Boudreaux's second-story corner office afforded him a wide view of Scipio Creek. Just below were the docks where his company's shrimp boats were moored. Off to the southeast, Big Towhead Island, and just beyond it, the John Gorrie Bridge over to Eastpoint.

Boudreaux tended to prefer working at his seafood wholesaling business in the late afternoon or early evening, especially in the summer months, when it didn't get dark until almost nine. He had decent people managing things, and the work he preferred to do himself could be accomplished in just a few hours, if that. Some days, he didn't come in at all.

At sixty-three, he looked decades younger than he should have, given how hard he'd worked on the shrimp boats and the oyster beds earlier in life. His hair was tinged with silver just above the ears, but it was thick and shiny and still mostly golden-brown. He was naturally tan and not prone to wrinkles, a fact for which he could thank his Spanish mother. But it was his eyes that garnered the most attention; they were the surreal blue of Bahamian water, and when they focused on someone, that person became the only person in the room.

For women, this was intoxicating, for men it was more frightening than alluring. Bennett Boudreaux was friend to local and state politicians, donor to many charities, and the wealthiest man in Franklin County. He was also suspected of shady dealings, the convenient disappearances of inconvenient people, and more than one killing. He'd never been arrested for or charged with any of these things, due to lack of evidence, and lack of motivation. His relationships with people in power were carefully cultivated and even more carefully tended. The same could be said of his relationships with the many people in the county who depended on him for their living. He might wear expensive cologne and hand-tailored pants, but he still had his callouses, he paid more than anyone else, and he'd been known to quietly take care of medical bills, past-due mortgage payments, and the occasional bail.

So, on the one hand, his Cajun Crawfish Festival was one of the highlights of the summer. On the other hand, no one ever forgot that he once brought a knife to a gunfight and won.

He stared out at the water, which was just beginning to take on a yellow cast from the waning sun. He watched a pelican boot an indignant seagull from an old piling and tried to block the tinny sound of suppressed noise behind him, but he couldn't help glancing over his shoulder.

Miss Evangeline, not a day over one hundred, sat on a leather loveseat across the room. Her new iPad was clutched in her claw-like hands, and the white wires of her earbuds dangled beneath her chin. Her head was wrapped in a purple bandana, and Coke bottle lenses in wide, round frames overwhelmed her tiny face. Every thirty seconds, she plucked a shelled pistachio from a bag that hung from a hook on her aluminum walker.

A Creole woman from Boudreaux's hometown of Houma, LA, Miss Evangeline had been his father's housekeeper and the woman who'd raised young Bennett. Now her daughter Amelia ran the house, and Miss Evangeline continued to raise Boudreaux. He'd always said she was the only woman he'd ever really loved, despite the fact that he'd been married for thirty-five years. The best year of his marriage of convenience had been this past one; his lovely wife had moved back to Louisiana, presumably to fester, spend money, and choose her next husband.

He looked back out the window as the ousted seagull came back with a beefier friend and proceeded to try to taunt the pelican from his perch. The pelican considered him serenely, like a kindly science teacher would a struggling student.

"Ooooh, law!" Miss Evangeline suddenly barked. Boudreaux looked over at her. "I need you tote me to the picture show!" she yelled in that way people do when they're wearing headphones.

"What for?" Boudreaux asked mildly.

"Speak up, boy!"

He pointed at his ear. "Take the earphones out."

"What's wrong the ear? Lemme slow the TV." She pushed one of the buttons on the iPad. "What you say?"

"I asked why I needed to take you to the movies," he said patiently. "What's wrong with renting a movie on that thing?"

"That ain't no good, no," she said, shaking her head. "Denzel got a new movie. The maxi pad ain't no good for Denzel. Got to see the big movie, me."

Boudreaux died just a little inside. The last time he'd taken her to an actual theatre, the teenaged boy behind the concessions counter had ended up bursting into tears. He'd rather have surgery than take her to another movie. Last week, she'd forgotten that Ronald Reagan was dead. Hopefully, this week she'd forget that Denzel Washington was still alive.

"When we go the house?" Miss Evangeline barked.

Boudreaux was minding his nanny while her daughter Amelia was at the dentist in Port St. Joe. He looked at his watch. It was quarter to seven, and Amelia's appointment had been for five o'clock, so she should be back any time now.

"Amelia should be here shortly," he answered. "Would you like me to make you a cup of tea?"

"Don't need no tea, no," the woman answered, shaking her head. "Then I be up all night, me, listen to them cock-a-roaches bang theyself on the window screen till mornin'."

She looked back down at her iPad, and stuck her earbud back into her ear. The distant sounds of some TV show wafted across the room again. Boudreaux twisted his chair around to face the window as the sound of a diesel engine rose from the water below.

It was a sportfishing boat, a fairly new one. A man with a dirty-blond ponytail was at the helm on the flybridge.

Boudreaux stood up so that he could see the deck, and was surprised to see someone familiar. Sheriff Curtis Bledsoe looked around him before stepping down into the cabin. He was followed by an impressively-built man with sparse blond hair. Another man, larger and with dark hair the color of his sunglasses, was sitting on one of the deck boxes.

It wasn't at all uncommon for boaters from all over the Gulf Coast to spend time in Apalach, so the fact that the boat was unfamiliar didn't make it interesting. What was interesting was the fact that the sheriff was aboard. He'd once heard Bledsoe say that, being from Orlando, he was much more comfortable on land than on the water.

As the boat passed, Boudreaux's gaze dropped to the transom. It took a moment of squinting for him to make out the name of the boat. The *Lucky Lady*, out of Bradenton, FL. Not exactly imaginative, but then he didn't think Bledsoe attracted imaginative or even intelligent friends. He knew Bledsoe to be a close pal of Governor Spaulding, and he knew Governor Spaulding to be close pals with some pretty shady people; drug dealers in particular. Boudreaux loathed drugs, despised what they did to families, what they did to communities. If there were a legal season on drug dealers, Boudreaux would go out and buy a whole new wardrobe of camo. Hand-tailored, of course, but intended for practical use.

He stood there at the plate glass window, watching the boat as it headed out toward the bay. It was almost at the bridge when Miss Evangeline piped up behind him.

"Why we got to wait Amelia? We go on and go the house."

"We can't. Amelia has your booster seat," he told the window distractedly.

"Amelia lose what?"

"Never mind," he said, turning away from the window. "I'm sure she'll be here in a few minutes."

CHAPTER

FIVE

The gravel and broken oyster shells that made up their driveway crunched beneath the tires of Wyatt's pick-up. The driveway paralleled Hwy 98 for a bit, then jutted left toward the water and the house. Sabal palms and palmettos waved at Wyatt as he passed, rustling in a good evening breeze. It wouldn't be true dark for another two hours, but the steel-shaded cloud cover made sundown seem imminent.

Wyatt was surprised to see that Sky's aged light blue Toyota truck was the only vehicle parked at the end of the driveway, but then he remembered that Maggie was picking up the cake.

Their portly dog Coco, half-Lab and half-Catahoula, stood at attention on the front porch, already smiling. When Wyatt opened his door, she jogged down the front steps to meet him halfway, tags jingling and tail wagging.

"Hey, Coco," Wyatt said, bending to pat her as he walked toward the house. "Where's your mom?" he asked.

Next to the front door was a doggy door that actually served as a cat door when Maggie was growing up. It was too small for Coco, but just right for Stoopid, who tried not to go outside voluntarily, lest someone actually make him stay out.

He popped his head out through the flap, like a meerkat from its den, and laid a loud but mangled crow on Wyatt.

"Stoopid, who are you telling?" Wyatt asked as he stepped onto the porch. "We're all expecting me."

Coco followed him into the house, and Wyatt followed the sound of voices to the kitchen, trailed by both dog and rooster.

Sky was making a salad at the island and Kyle was busy setting the table when Wyatt and his entourage arrived in the kitchen. Kyle was that kind of handsome that bordered on pretty, with his shiny black hair, bright green eyes, and long lashes. Wyatt had known him since he was a toddler and thought he might possibly be the coolest kid he'd ever known. The boy looked up from the silverware in his hand.

"Hey, Wyatt."

"Hey, guy. How's it going?"

Kyle shrugged, teenaged vernacular for pretty much everything, Wyatt had learned. "Okay," the boy answered. "Granddad and I are almost done with Grandma's table. It's turning out pretty cool."

"That's awesome," Wyatt said, setting his keys and wallet down on the counter. "Where's your mom?"

"I was gonna ask you," Sky answered.

Sky was the image of her mother, with her long, dark brown hair and her sharp green eyes. She had her hair pulled up in a ponytail and was wearing the Seminoles t-shirt she'd bought during her last campus visit. It made him want to go dig out his Crimson Tide cap.

"I haven't talked to her since lunch," Wyatt told her, snatching a fallen crouton from the cutting board. It was his favorite salad vegetable.

"I talked to her around five-thirty," Sky said. "She was on her way to get the cake, I think, but now her phone's dead. I was going to ask her if we were out of parmesan cheese, but I found it."

"Okay," Wyatt said. "She probably decided to sneak a latte without bringing us any."

Sky opened her mouth to say something but was interrupted by a cacophony of feathers and poor coordination as Stoopid landed on the island and gave the salad bowl his best come-hither look.

"I will seriously give you such a flick in the beak," Sky said steadily.

Stoopid warbled out some argument for why he should be permitted to climb into the salad bowl, and Sky picked up a stump of Romaine and dropped it onto the floor. "Go amuse yourself," she said to Stoopid, and he flapped to the floor and set himself to disassembling his treat.

Wyatt pulled out his new iPhone, which still felt odd in his hand. "Twenty bucks says she's sneaking coffee. Show me the thingy for finding her phone again."

Sky gave him half an eyeroll. "I don't understand you. It's like trying to teach a squid to ride a bicycle."

"You're precious," Wyatt said.

"Yeah. It doesn't matter, anyway." She tossed some sliced mushrooms into the salad bowl. "Her phone's dead."

"Still? It was dead an hour ago."

Sky shrugged again. "I don't know what to tell you. She'll be here. You know how she is about company."

"Yeah," Wyatt answered, starting to loosen his tie. "I'm gonna go take a shower. When she gets here, sniff her breath. Twenty bucks."

On his way out of the kitchen, he nearly trod upon Stoopid, who goose-stepped across his path in pursuit of his rolling Romaine stump.

⚓ ⚓ ⚓

Maggie came to in an unfamiliar head. It was tiny, even by marine standards, clearly meant to be used as a day head, so she guessed she was on the sport-fisher she'd seen at the day dock.

She was sitting on the floor, with her back propped up against the head itself and her feet against the bulkhead next to the closed door. The head vibrated with the power of the diesel engines.

Once she realized what she was leaning on, she shifted her body. Her head pulsed, with a particularly painful pounding in her temple, as she reached up and grabbed onto the edge of the small, stainless sink.

Her first attempt to pull herself to a standing position was met with more intense pounding and a lack of effective response from her legs. She might as well have had a pair of pool noodles for prostheses. She regrouped for a moment, then managed to pull herself up, albeit a bit shakily.

She leaned against the sink for a minute, waiting for the pounding in her temple to subside a bit. As it did, she tested first one leg, and then the other, pressing each foot against the floor to flex her leg muscles.

She could hear a man's voice beyond the head door. He was speaking so quietly she couldn't make out what he was saying, but she recognized the voice as belonging to the man with the wispy blond hair, self-satisfied smile, and decent right hook. Noel, he'd said his name was Noel.

Maggie reached over and depressed the stainless lever that served as a door-knob. It moved, but the door to the head did not. Most boats had hooks or sliding locks that secured their doors while underway, and Maggie supposed someone had secured this one. It was a flimsy door, and she could probably kick it open after a few tries, but there wasn't much point in that. The men out in the main cabin would just sit there and wait for her to bust through, then either shoot her or hit her with the Taser again.

The Taser. Curtis Bledsoe had tasered her. She'd never particularly liked the man, had disliked him quite a bit for the first few months he'd been sheriff, but she had a hard time with the idea that he would actually do her harm, especially since he'd done so much for Dwight and his family after Dwight's shooting. But harm her he had, and she knew that his doing that had sealed her fate. There was nowhere good to go from there.

She could still hear men's voices out in the main cabin, and once she knew she was steady on her feet, she let go of the sink and leaned toward the door. She pressed her ear to the door-jamb and listened.

The voices were muffled, and it was clear that the men on the other side of the door were watching their volume, but she could catch snatches of the conversation.

"…another fifteen minutes…waiting," said the man who called himself Noel.

Bledsoe responded, his voice subdued. "…best thing…office…reschedule."

"We wait," Noel said clearly and firmly.

Maggie heard a grumbling answer from one of the other men, then everyone fell silent.

She didn't have to check her holsters to know they were too light. Her service weapon was gone from her side holster, and her back-up was no longer on her ankle. Even her keys were gone from her back pocket.

She looked around the darkening head for something she might use to defend herself, but the tiny medicine cabinet held only a couple of packets of Dramamine and a bottle of Wal-Mart brand aspirin. The cupboard beneath the sink stocked only a few rolls of marine toilet paper. She doubted the men had hurriedly cleared out the head before locking her in it, so she guessed that the boat wasn't used for any kind of extended cruising.

Where were they headed? If they were sticking close to the coastline, she might have half a chance to swim to shore or at least tread water long enough for a passing boat to pick her up. If she managed to get herself overboard—the thought of which made her sick to her stomach. She usually didn't feel the effects of her PTSD very much, and even when she did, she didn't mind some of them. But this was different. The sharks were different. Being in the water was different.

She stood on tiptoe at the tiny porthole beside the head. She had a limited range of vision, so she couldn't tell exactly where they were, but they were out in the bay. There was a decent chop going, though it wasn't unmanageable. The water was a darkened steel beneath the overcast sky.

She might be able to swim to shore from here, given the opportunity. The weather being what it was, her chances of being picked up by a passing fishing boat were even slimmer than usual. She gave herself a mental shake. The reality was, she was probably going to be dead before she hit the water.

She looked around the head more carefully, her eyes scanning every surface and then the bulkheads. She stepped over to the small, empty towel rack over the head itself. Two corroded screws fixed it to the bulkhead. She checked the pockets of her cargo pants in case she might have a stray coin, but she didn't.

She heard the men speaking again as she stuck her short-trimmed thumbnail into the head of one of the screws and tried to loosen it. After several tries, her thumbnail broke and she hadn't budged the screw. It had been a long shot, anyway. Most likely, the screw was too short to help her.

She went back to leaning against the sink. There was nothing in the head that she could see using as a weapon. She was going to have to hope something presented itself whenever they got around to taking her out of the head.

CHAPTER
SIX

Sheriff Curtis Bledsoe nervously drummed his fingers against the triangular fiberglass table in front of the settee. He could feel droplets of perspiration sliding down his spine, and he pressed his back against the settee to keep himself from scratching at them.

Across the table, the man Bledsoe knew only as Noel slowly turned his iPhone around and around on the table. The other man, whose name Bledsoe didn't know, sat on the other settee across the cabin, seemingly staring into some void.

Bledsoe was almost physically sick of the pounding of his own heart. He'd met with Noel before, had even met with Noel's boss, Gavin Betancourt, but he'd done so on land, with his car at hand in case he needed to leave. Now he was on a boat he wasn't controlling and couldn't operate, headed out into the Gulf to meet the dealers from Gainesville, dealers he didn't know. He'd been uncomfortable with this plan from the get-go, but it was the way Governor Troy Spaulding wanted it, and he'd been appointed sheriff here so he could do what Spaulding wanted.

But now he was on his way out to the Gulf with guys he didn't trust to meet other guys he didn't know and reassure them that, because of him, Franklin County would be a safe place for the two parties to conduct business; Gavin's people selling their wares to the Gainesville group, who would distribute them throughout the Panhandle.

Worse than the uncertainty regarding these two groups of men was the certainty of Maggie Hamilton's presence in the head. Even now, Bledsoe was having a hard time believing that he'd been that stupid. Right up until the moment he'd hit her with the Taser, everything could still have worked out, but he'd seen the distrust in her eyes and he'd panicked.

Now Maggie's fate was a foregone conclusion, and while he might have sold his moral compass a long time ago, he wasn't so far gone that he couldn't feel regret or shame.

He resented the Hamiltons too much to actually like them; resented their offhanded knowledge of their place in the world, their easy acceptance of approval, respect and community, as though they were to be expected. But he didn't hate them enough to want it taken from them.

Noel's brows leaned against each other as he looked pointedly at Bledsoe's hyperactive fingers.

"Would it be possible for you to stop?" he asked Bledsoe drily.

Bledsoe's fingers stilled as Noel's phone buzzed. The man picked it up.

"Yes, Gavin," he answered.

Bledsoe could just hear the man on the other end speaking. Noel listened patiently until the man had said his piece.

"I understand," Noel said then. "What would you like me to do now?" He listened for another moment, and Bledsoe strained, unsuccessfully, to do the same.

"I'll take care of it," Noel said finally. "We'll have to refuel somewhere along the way, but we'll be back in the morning."

He disconnected the call, set the phone back down on the table, and looked at Bledsoe.

"Our prospective partners have opted to reschedule for an as yet unknown time," he said smoothly. "They're uncomfortable with our cargo."

It took an act of will for Bledsoe to not nervously lick his lip. "So we're going back?"

"Eventually. First, we have to offload your friend."

"She's not my friend," Bledsoe said, keeping his voice unconcerned.

"Well, if she was, she certainly isn't now."

⚓ ⚓ ⚓

Wyatt ran a hand through his still-damp hair as he looked out over the back-yard. The water beyond their dock had turned a dark gray, reflecting the cloud cover overhead, and the sun was beginning to retreat in earnest. He looked at his watch. 7:15.

"Probably still quarter after seven," Dwight said quietly beside him. His cane was leaning against the deck rail, and although he kept one hand on the rail, Dwight was basically standing on his own. Now he just needed to gain back the ten pounds he couldn't spare but had lost anyway. His Adam's apple was bigger than his biceps.

Wyatt threw him a look, but it was half-hearted. "You know Maggie. She's a control freak when it comes to cooking and having company and what-ever. There's no pleasant reason for her to be late without calling."

"Reckon not," Dwight answered. "But it could just be a call no one else was handy for."

"Maybe," Wyatt answered, but he wasn't even trying to sound convincing to himself. He had a hinky feeling, and it made him more nervous by the minute. It didn't help that the sky was all stormy and the wind had picked up, just like it did in movies when something bad was about to happen but the writers thought the audience was too stupid to pick that up on their own.

"Crap!" Wyatt said suddenly, putting a palm over his eyes for a moment.

"What?"

"The radio. I forgot about the radio." He set his beer down. "I'm gonna go call her on the radio, see what's keeping her."

He started for the deck stairs but stopped as he heard Dwight's cane clumping behind him. "Forget it, Dwight. The rest of us will be inside eating dinner by the time you Festus your way out to the driveway. I'll be right back."

"You don't have to be hurtful, though," Dwight said quietly as Wyatt headed for the side of the house.

Wyatt walked to the side yard, then through it and around the garage that was used for storage. His worn deck shoes crunched beneath him as he moved from grass to oyster shells. He made a point of not rushing to his truck and the radio inside. Rushing would make it seem like he was more worried than he was ready to be.

He opened the driver's door, picked up the radio and keyed the mic. "Franklin 101 to Franklin 103." He lifted his thumb and waited a moment, then tried again. "Franklin 101 to Franklin 103, come in."

He waited another moment, then hung up the handset and slammed his door shut. Dwight was standing on the front steps.

"I walked through the house," Dwight said. "All Festus-like."

⚓　⚓　⚓

Maggie heard footsteps coming toward the head, and she took her ear from the door. She hadn't been able to make anything out over the diesel engines anyway. She backed up against the little stainless sink as the door opened and the big guy with the brown hair and vacant look glared in at her.

"Come on," he said, holding out his hand.

Maggie couldn't exactly do anything else, unless she wanted to throw herself to the floor and beg, which she did not, so she pushed off from the sink and headed for the door. The man grabbed her elbow as she reached him and pulled her the rest of the way out into the main cabin.

The fact that they hadn't bothered to restrain her in any way was almost insulting. They weren't afraid of her because she was a female, and it rankled her, even while she knew that being offended was the least of her problems. Too, there really wasn't much need to restrain her; even if her hand-to-hand combat skills were as awesome as TV-watchers would think, she couldn't realistically take on all of these guys. Only Noel, Bledsoe and the guy with the personality were below, but there was at least one more at the helm, and Maggie heard the engines shut down.

Maggie's only real chance was to get herself off the boat and into the water, but they'd been moving for at least an hour that she knew of, and they weren't in Scipio Creek anymore. The idea of going into the Gulf, or even the bay, made her feel nauseous. It wasn't as frightening as getting shot, which was probably the plan, but it was scary nonetheless. If she got the chance to jump overboard, she hoped her fear wouldn't make her hesitate long enough to get a bullet in the back of her head.

The man named Noel frowned at her, then stood and led the way up to the deck. Maggie glared at Bledsoe as the quiet guy led her past the settee, but Bledsoe avoided her gaze and stepped out to bring up the rear. As they made their way up the companionway steps, Maggie heard the electric windlass kick in, and lengths of anchor chain rattling at the bow.

When they got up on deck, Maggie saw that there was another man there, with dark brown hair and dark sunglasses, even though the overcast sky made it even darker than it would normally be about now. The guy leading Maggie had her by the left wrist, and she hurriedly glanced at her old Timex, surprised to see that it was quarter after seven.

She was also surprised to see that they were a lot further out than she'd have guessed, and she realized they must have left the dock almost immediately after she'd been knocked unconscious. She looked over her shoulder, first one way, then the other, and her heart sank when she realized that they were out of sight of land. Even St. George Island was too far to see. They could be anywhere.

Then something caught her eye off the port side, and when she looked, she realized it was the "C" Tower, one of several structures, roughly twenty feet tall, that belonged to the military, but were popular as vertical reefs for area fishermen. It was eight or so miles straight out from the cut, a manmade channel between St. George and Little St. George Islands. She hadn't been out this far in some time, but she'd been out there when fishing with her daddy, and back in her twenties, when she used to crew for David on their shrimp boat a couple of nights a week. In fact, they weren't that far from his "Golden Hole," his favorite shrimping spot and final resting place.

Dear God, don't let my kids have to deal with both of their parents being out here, she thought. *Any-place but here. Any month but July.* But she honestly couldn't see any way out of dying tonight, dying here.

She glanced quickly around the deck, looking for something, anything, that would make her feel like she had options. She noticed that the men had gone to the trouble of sticking a couple of rods into the holders on the stern. There was even a ten-gallon bucket of bait next to one of them, and an open cooler with at least three whole redfish lying in the ice. They were bull redfish, good-sized.

Maggie figured they probably picked them up from a fisherman or wholesaler somewhere, but the set-up would look pretty good if they got boarded by the Coast Guard for any reason. The only off thing was that those nice big bull redfish liked lures or shrimp, not the huge chunks of fish sitting in the bait bucket.

Noel gestured toward the starboard gunwale, and the big guy pulled her toward it, then let go, but he stood nearby. Maggie leaned against the rail, which came to just above her backside. Not much, as deterrents to accidental overboards went.

She looked over at Bledsoe, who was standing behind Noel, one hand on the port rail. The guy in the sunglasses remained seated on a deck locker beside him. Bledsoe had been looking at her, but when she caught his eye he quickly glanced away. Coward.

"Officer, I'm afraid you've really screwed up our day," Noel said in an almost-friendly voice. Maggie didn't answer. "Although, I have to say that Curtis here probably needs to take the majority of the blame. "We might have all gone back to our own business if he hadn't been so hasty."

Maggie looked over his shoulder at Bledsoe. This time, he didn't look away immediately, but it didn't take him long.

"I understand you've had previous dealings with my employer, Gavin Betancourt," Noel continued.

That name startled Maggie just a bit. Betancourt was a big-time drug dealer over in Tampa. He'd been a suspect, albeit the wrong suspect, in the murder of her friend Axel Blackwell's ex-wife the previous year.

"He'd be interested in knowing why you were at that dock today, ma'am."

Maggie shook her head. "No reason. I was down the block and saw my boss's car." There was no real point in answering Noel; the response was just automatic.

"I see." He looked over his shoulder at Bledsoe, then back at Maggie. "Not because your department's interested in what Curtis does in his spare time?"

"No."

Maggie's brain was spinning from one thought to another. How to let someone know that Gavin Betancourt was behind her probable death. Whether she'd survive jumping overboard, terror and heart attacks aside. Why Betancourt and Bledsoe were working together, because clearly, they were. Each thought or question lasted a millisecond, because she couldn't slow her thinking.

She watched as Noel walked over to the cooler and bent to pick up a redfish. He straightened, cradling the fish's back in one hand as he reached into his front pocket with the other. He withdrew a switchblade, popped it open, and smiled at Maggie.

"I'm not sure I believe you."

He glanced over at the man next to Maggie, and before she even had time to look, he'd pushed her in the chest with such force that she felt like she'd been punched.

She hit the water hard, gracelessly, on her back, her legs in the air, like she was going SCUBA diving. Thanks to years of living on the water, she had taken an instinctive breath as she fell, but she still got a good bit of salt water up her nose before she righted herself and surfaced.

She took another gulp of air, more from fear than from physical need. She was in the water. The Gulf. At least eight miles out, in the dark, in water that was seventy to eighty feet deep. Not deep by boating standards, but bottomless if you had no boat.

Noel stood at the starboard rail. With the light of the boat above and behind him, it was hard to make out his face, but there was a smile in his voice.

"How good a swimmer are you, Lieutenant?"

Maggie didn't answer. She wasn't sure if she could have. Her chest felt like it was closing in on itself, and her brain seemed to focus on the vulnerability of every one of her limbs and digits. He bent down, then straightened again.

"Let me rephrase that," he said mildly. "How *fast* a swimmer are you?"

He raised his arm and something was lobbed toward her. It landed with a plop about two feet to her right and sunk before she could see what it was. He raised his arm again, and this time she saw the shape of what was coming. It was the back third of a fish, its tail evident if not distinct as it sailed through the air and landed in front of her. Chum. He was chumming the water, and Maggie felt a panic so profound that she stopped treading water for just a moment.

Noel started to speak but she missed it, as she sank almost to her forehead before jerking her limbs into action again. She surfaced again as another large chunk of fish landed nearby.

"Were you following your boss, lieutenant?"

Maggie tried to regulate her breathing. Answering him was pointless. It didn't matter that she just happened to be curious. It wouldn't make any difference that she wasn't surveilling Bledsoe. These people weren't going to pull her back aboard and give her a ride home. She remembered the cold, sickly certainty that he was going to shoot her in the back of the head. She wished he had.

Her terror, rational or not, was a palpable thing, like fire or cold steel. Maggie had been brave at times in her life, she knew she had. She had faced gunfire and been shot. She had been attacked more times than she could remember at that moment. She'd gotten her kids through the worst hurricane of her lifetime. She had a little collateral damage, but she'd survived being raped as a teen. She knew she was strong and capable of feeling courage, but she was not capable of feeling it now. The one unthinkable thing was here, now.

They're coming, they're coming, they're coming kept churning through her mind, fast and relentless. Of course, they were coming. This part of the Gulf was loaded with sharks. Mostly bulls and tigers, but also the occasional Great White. People fished them right from shore, sometimes catching sharks that were over six feet long, right on the beach. As she struggled to stay afloat and keep from losing her mind, Maggie could almost feel the crunch of teeth through bone as a shark took her foot, could see her own blood swirling around her in a terrible cloud as a shark bit down on her thigh and pulled her down and down.

"Answer my question, and you can die much more quickly," Noel said.

Maggie snapped back to the here and now.

"No, she wasn't following me," Bledsoe piped up from behind him. "I told you, she just happened to see my car."

"And you just happened to be stupid enough to Taser her," Noel snapped, that creepy edge back in his voice. He turned back to Maggie, who was starting to feel the weight of her hiking boots. "Were you following him? Were you *told* to follow him?"

Another chunk of fish landed to Maggie's right. Stupidly, she reached out to shove it away from her, but it had already sunk out of sight in the dark water.

"Were you told to follow him?" Noel asked, sounding a bit angrier. He was losing patience.

Maggie was about to yell an answer, though she didn't know what that answer should be, when she saw Bledsoe move suddenly. He was in the boat's deck lights, and she could see his face. He didn't look angry, or scared, or determined. He looked resigned. Reconciled.

She registered a moment of surprise that she was capable of noticing that, and then Bledsoe was reaching for Noel, and the guy with the ponytail was reaching for a weapon.

He stepped behind Bledsoe, slapped a hand on his shoulder, and Maggie heard the shot. A dark shadow blossomed over Bledsoe's chest, and his eyes met hers for just a second before the gunman shoved him over the side.

He went in head first, arms spread, sinking a few feet and then floating back up to the surface, facedown. Maggie instinctively turned him over. His eyes were open, staring vacantly at the leaden sky.

Noel whipped around to face his man. "I didn't authorize you to do that!" he snapped.

"He was going for you."

"With what?"

Maggie tried to get her terrified brain to change focus. She couldn't think about the fact that she was treading water miles from shore, in seventy feet of water, in the Gulf. The Gulf that she used to love so much before her phobia of sharks drove her from it.

She had to get away. She needed to get away from the chum. She needed to get away from the body. She needed to do that now.

"Ah!" she screamed out, then lifted an arm and let herself drop beneath the surface of the water.

She forced herself down several feet, below the reach of the deck lights. She needed to get over to the port side. For the first few moments, they would be focusing on the starboard side. The hull was just a darker shape in dark water, but she could make it out. She felt her left contact lens become dislodged. She blinked twice and it was gone.

She figured the beam, or width, of the boat was about twelve or thirteen feet, and she was about seven feet away when she went under. Ordinarily, twenty feet was nothing. When she was younger, she could very easily swim three times as far underwater. But she hadn't been underwater in a long time, and she was scared, and she was wearing boots.

She swam beneath the boat, praying her natural buoyancy wouldn't lift her. She was only about five feet beneath it. She swam using a careful crawl stroke, trying to override her fear in order to stroke as efficiently and effectively as possible. If buoyancy took over, she'd bump against the hull and they'd wait for a chance to shoot her. If she ran out of breath and panicked, bumping against the hull, they'd wait for a chance to shoot her, or she'd just drown. If they decided to leave now, they'd probably run her over.

At the forefront of her mind, though, was the fact that a bloody body and several bloody chunks of fish were just a few yards behind her. The thought made her want to thrash, to scream, to pop to the surface and scramble up the port side of the boat to be shot. The sharks would still get her, but maybe she wouldn't know.

Instead, she forced her strong legs to frog kick in spite of the boots, forced herself to dive a foot or so deeper despite her need for air. Once she cleared the hull, she fought the instinct to surface immediately. She swam a good ten feet farther, as far as she could manage on the air she had. It was only about three feet past the pool of light cast by the boat, but it would have to do. Then her task became dropping her feet and easing her body to the surface, instead of scrambling for it.

Her chest felt like someone was holding a heavy, heated weight against it, and her temples pounded, but she stroked gently, and when her head broke the surface she gulped the clean, cool air as silently as she could.

From her position, with only her head above water, she couldn't see the men on the boat, but she could see a flashlight strafing the water astern of the boat, then swinging back toward the starboard side. She couldn't make out what anyone was saying, but more than one man was speaking.

Suddenly, one of the men cursed loudly, and there was a whooshing sound on the other side of the boat.

"Did you *see* that?" one of the voices yelled.

Complete and total terror enveloped Maggie. She knew what he saw. She knew what she'd heard. A shark or sharks had found the chum, or the body, or both.

Her breathing became shallow and unhelpful. Her face tingled around the edges and every follicle above water expanded. In just a few seconds, her limbs started to feel numb, though she was still treading water.

Away.

She needed to be away, more than she needed to give vent to her abject terror. The idea of putting her face back in the water was almost paralyzing, even though she'd known before that the sharks would be there, *were* there. But now she knew how close they were, and she knew that more were coming.

The shark who'd caused such excitement had actually done her a favor, by making it seem more likely that she'd been pulled under. Even so, the men still might move to the port side to search for her. She needed to not be on the surface until she was out of range of their flashlights, at least. But which way?

She looked up at the sky, but the clouds were low and thick. There was no moon, and there were no stars. The lack of moon might work in her favor at the moment but would be a hindrance later. If there was a later.

Get your act together, Maggie. Think. Why are you looking for celestial bodies? Go back the way you came.

She took a long, silent breath, blew it out just as quietly, and dove.

CHAPTER
SEVEN

WEDNESDAY, JULY 11TH 7:25 PM

William put the new money drawer into the cash register, then shut the drawer and locked the register.

"Are you coming?" he called.

"I'm coming," Robert called back.

"Don't forget the lunch bag."

"I won't forget the lunch bag."

"I'm going to the car to start the AC," William said as he gathered his Filofax, his water bottle and his phone. "Hurry up, the Crock Pot's probably wondering if we're coming back!"

"I said I'm coming," Robert called. As he did, the light went out in back, and William could hear the back door lock.

He opened the front door and let it close behind him, the little brass bell tinkling farewell. Then he walked around the side to the small gravel parking lot. He was surprised to see the little sheriff's Jeep parked there, right next to their Mini-Cooper. He looked at his phone. It was almost seven-thirty. She'd said her company was coming at seven.

He frowned as he walked around the back of the Jeep and over to the driver's door. He peered in to see that a cake box sat on the passenger seat, and the floral arrangement they'd made for her table was quickly wilting atop it. An iPhone sat on the console, plugged into the charger.

William set his things down on the roof of their car, then picked up his phone. He thumbed his recent calls page and then tapped on Robert's number. Robert answered immediately.

"I got the lunch bag," he said.

"Never mind that. Get out here immediately!" William demanded. "Something is amiss!"

"Now what?" Robert asked.

William heard it on the phone and also behind him. Robert was just stepping into the parking lot. "Look at this!" he said, gesturing at the Jeep.

"What?" Robert asked, still talking into the phone.

"Hang up the phone, idjit," William said.

Robert came to stand beside William and slid his phone into the back pocket of his cargo shorts. "What's your problem?"

"This is my problem," William snapped. "Her car is still here, with a cake that's probably turned to pudding, and our beautiful arrangement just wasting away. And her cell phone is sitting right there in the open, with her doors unlocked."

"Maybe she got called away."

"On what, the streetcar?"

"Downtown is three blocks in any direction," Robert said. "Clearly she walked."

"I don't think so. I don't think so at all." William put his hands on his hips. "I think there's been criminal mischief, right here. Right across the street from the Chamber of Commerce, for Pete's sake!"

"She's running an errand or something."

William thumbed open his contacts list.

"Who are you calling?" Robert asked.

William waved him away as he tapped on a contact, then waited for an answer. "Hello, Sheriff's Department?"

"Oh, heavens to murgatroyd," Robert muttered.

"This is William the florist. William with a 'W'. You need to send someone over here to Commerce Street." He listened a few seconds. "Because I think somebody's made off with the little sheriff. No, the other one. Maggie Hamilton."

William answered a few more questions, then hung up the phone. He caught Robert's disdainful look and raised his eyebrows in indignation.

"Don't give me that look! I know something queer when I see it."

$$\text{⚓ ⚓ ⚓}$$

Wyatt leaned against the island as he picked at the crispy edges of the pan of lasagna. Dwight leaned against the sink, finishing his second beer, while his wife Amy, Sky, and Kyle sat at the kitchen table eating their salads.

Wyatt had called the office to see if Maggie had been called out for something. She hadn't. He had thought about calling her parents, but he knew she hadn't driven all the way out there when they were expecting Dwight and Amy, and he didn't want to scare Gray and Georgia unnecessarily. He was seriously contemplating getting in his truck and driving around to look for his wife when his phone rang. It was the Sheriff's Office, but it was the dispatch extension, not Maggie's. His heart rate picked up just a little.

"This is Wyatt," he answered.

"Boss, it's Lenny in dispatch."

"What's up, Lenny?"

"Well, most likely nothing, but those guys that own the flower shop on Commerce found Maggie's Jeep in their parking lot and they were worried because she left their shop like an hour ago. A little paranoid if you ask me, but we sent a unit from PD over there and nobody can find Maggie. Everything okay? You talk to her?"

"No, her phone's dead."

"According to Lon from PD, her phone's on the charger in her car. You think everything's okay, or what?"

"No, not really," Wyatt answered quietly. "I'll be down there in just a minute."

He hung up and looked over at Dwight.

"I heard," Dwight said, putting his beer bottle in the trash can. "You got that thing turned up kinda high."

"What's going on?" Sky asked.

All three of the people at the table were staring at him. He sighed. "Probably nothing. You know your mom; she gets caught up."

"Yeah, she gets caught up in making sure everything's perfect when she's cooking dinner for people," Sky said drily, but there was worry in her eyes. "What's going on?" she repeated.

"It probably really is nothing," Wyatt answered as he grabbed his keys, phone and weapon from the basket by the back door. "If something bad had happened in town, we would have heard about it."

"Where are you going?" Kyle asked.

"Down to Commerce Street," Wyatt answered. "Your mom's Cherokee is by the flower shop."

"I'll go with," Dwight said. He looked over at Amy. "That okay with you, baby?"

"Yeah, go on," she said. "I'll hang out with the kids."

"You don't have to come; it's nothing," Wyatt said.

"Then why're you taking your flip flops off?" Dwight asked.

"Just shut up and come on."

CHAPTER

EIGHT

Despite the fact that Wyatt and Maggie's house was on the outskirts of town, it was still only two miles away from Commerce Street, and Wyatt and Dwight pulled up to the curb behind an Apalach PD cruiser just five minutes after Wyatt had gotten the call.

There were two cars in the parking lot: Maggie's Jeep and a Mini-Cooper. William and Robert were standing between the two, talking to Sgt. Lon Woodman, an African-American man who stood an inch or so taller than even Wyatt. He had an easy, languid way about him, and a warm smile, that belied his willingness and ability to stomp pretty much anyone or anything.

He smiled at Wyatt now, his hands on his hips, as Wyatt and Dwight made their way to him, Dwight just a few steps behind.

"Hey, Wyatt," Lon said, his voice low and smooth as molasses.

"Hey, Lon," Wyatt said back, looking at Maggie's Jeep. Something about it being there, when he didn't know where she was, made little spider feet go up his spine.

"So, you haven't talked to Maggie? You don't know where she is?" Lon asked.

"Not since around four," Wyatt answered. "She was supposed to pick up a cake and be home probably before me. Dwight here was coming over for dinner."

"Cake's in the car, man."

Wyatt opened the driver's door.

"She was here just an hour or so ago," William said. "We made her that arrangement for the dinner table."

Wyatt reached down and flipped the lever on the side of the seat. It *zinged* back to the farthest position, revealing Maggie's small purse. More like a wallet with a strap, really. She wasn't much of a girly-girl. As long as she had room for her ID, her debit card and some lip balm, she seemed pretty happy.

He reached down and picked up the small blue purse. He unsnapped it to find everything there that he expected to see.

"That's worrying," William said quietly.

"Could you not?" Robert hissed.

Wyatt slid into the driver's seat, put the purse on the console, and picked up the iPhone. He knew the passcode, but it didn't matter; the phone was plugged in but dead.

He pulled the charger cord out of the lighter adapter. No wonder. They had six or seven white charger cables in the house, and none of them could remember to throw out the one that didn't work anymore. He was holding it in his hand. The wires peeked out from their plastic covering at the port end.

He put the phone back down. "Hey, Dwight? Can you grab my charger out of the truck?"

"Yeah, Boss."

Dwight moved off, and Wyatt moved the flowers and opened the lid of the cake box. The detective shield Maggie had asked Kirk to create was looking kind of warped, starting to melt into the chocolate frosting. He closed the box and looked up at Lon and the flower guys.

"Did she seem okay when you saw her?" he asked William.

"Yes, she was fine," William answered. "Kind of in a hurry to get home, which is why I got concerned."

"She said she needed to be home by seven," Robert said.

"She left a little before six-thirty or so," William added.

Wyatt bent to peer at the gas gauge. It was almost full. Around here, a tank of gas lasted forever, even in a Jeep.

As far as he could tell, the only things Maggie had taken with her when she got out of the car were her service weapon and her keys. Something wasn't right, but he wasn't sure what was wrong. He climbed out of the Jeep and looked at Lon.

"Nothing weird happened downtown?" he asked him.

"No, it's been quiet, man. Last thing I had was a speeding ticket over in front of the botanical garden."

"Okay."

Wyatt looked over his shoulder as Dwight approached, charger in hand.

"Here you go, Boss," Dwight said.

"Thanks, Dwight." Wyatt leaned back into the Jeep and plugged the phone back in with the new charger. Then he straightened back up to wait.

Lon glanced over at William and Robert before he spoke quietly. "Maggie workin' on anything?"

Wyatt shrugged. "Nothing big. She wrapped up that robbery case over in Eastpoint. She's getting ready to give her deposition for Dwight's shooting, but that's it."

Robert piped up politely. "Do you still need us? Our dinner's crusting over."

"Of course they need us," William chided. "We're eyewitnesses."

"To what?" Robert asked.

"We were the last people to see her."

"And now they know what we know," Robert said. "Cake, flowers, hurry, Jeep."

William opened his mouth, no doubt to set loose a scathing reply, but Wyatt intercepted. "We really appreciate you calling us, but it's best for you to go on home to your dinner," he said. "There's probably nothing wrong; just a little confusion."

William frowned. "Perhaps she hit her head, and she's wandering aimlessly."

"Well, then we'll find her in a few minutes," Wyatt said. "It's not like this is Atlanta."

"Come on, William, we need to get out of their way and let them do their thing," Robert said, tugging his partner toward the Mini-Cooper.

Wyatt, Dwight and Lon watched them pull out of the parking lot, then looked at each other. "You busy, Lon?" Wyatt asked.

"Yeah. Busy looking for Maggie," the man answered. "Where you want to start?"

"Let's split up and hit Tamara's, Hole in the Wall, Oyster City, anyplace that's open, especially with sidewalk seating. Maybe somebody saw her." He looked over at Dwight. "Do me a favor; call dispatch, see if we can get one more officer out here to help us look. Just drive around."

"What do you think's going on, boss?"

"I don't have any damn idea," Wyatt answered. He took off his cap to run a hand through his hair, then slapped it back onto his head. "But I want to know where Maggie is."

⚓   ⚓   ⚓

WEDNESDAY, JULY 11TH 8:30 PM

Once the rumbling sounds of the boat's diesels had quickly faded, there had been little sound other than the slap of the chop. Maggie had been in the water for what seemed like an hour, though it could have been two hours or twenty minutes. Her phobia of sharks had led her to believe she'd be dead within ten minutes of hitting the water, and the back of her mind registered surprise at her reprieve, however temporary it might prove to be.

She had unconsciously developed a pattern of swimming for ten or fifteen minutes, then treading water for five or ten, giving her shoulders and legs a chance to regroup or, at least, regroup enough to start swimming again.

She knew she wasn't going to be swimming to shore, beating her body into an eight or ten-mile swim to St. George Island, where she would rest on the sand for a few minutes before asking a tourist if she could borrow their phone. But she could get closer to home.

Her odds of being spotted by a shrimper or fisherman were better closer to shore, and really, why would she swim in any other direction? Regardless of whether she thought she could make it or not, she had no place to head but home.

She sighed and let her legs drop, let them hang beneath her as she swung her arms to loosen them, then started treading water again. She couldn't see land, couldn't see her home, but she knew where it was, and she faced it as though waiting for it to materialize on the horizon. It was starting to get dark in earnest, and she could just see a slightly lighter patch of darkness in the sky ahead.

There were just enough lights in Apalach, Eastpoint and on the island to create a very slight haze in the sky above them. She wasn't sure if she was facing Apalach exactly; she might be pointed more toward the island, but either way, she was pointed toward home, and she looked at the space where she knew it to be with a longing that she could physically feel.

Despite the fact that her eyes were already starting to feel scorched by the salt spray, she felt them warm with unshed tears, and her vision blurred for a moment. Home. Somewhere over there was home, and in it were her people. Her babies. Her husband and best friend. Her parents. Her sweet dog and her feckless rooster.

People swam the English Channel all the time. Granted, they were incredibly fit people who trained for long distance swimming in the open sea, and she was not, but she doubted that any Channel swimmer was more determined than a woman who wasn't ever going to see her children again unless she kept swimming.

Her legs felt like lead, and her thigh muscles twitched and quivered. Keeping her head above water would soon become impossible if she didn't get rid of the hiking boots that now felt like anvils at the ends of her legs.

The idea of being barefoot in the water was senselessly frightening. Logically, she knew that the thick leather offered her little protection against sharks. She also knew that the boots were going to exhaust her quickly, and that her subsequent drowning was more of a sure thing than being eaten by sharks.

The logical part of her brain, the part that reasoned, knew these things, but the more primitive part was screaming that she couldn't just let her feet dangle naked in the water.

She frog-kicked for a few more minutes, staring toward home and spitting out mouthfuls of salt water as small, gray-green waves hit the side of her face. She was doing her best not to swallow much of it. Her daddy had been with search and rescue for years. One of his best friends, Skip Shiver, who'd been sheriff years ago, was still the head of the volunteer search and rescue team. Maggie wasn't an expert on ocean survival, but she knew some basics.

Hypothermia was usually the biggest enemy of someone adrift in the water, but it was mid-July and the water temperature was in the seventies. Her core would still eventually reach that temperature if she was in the water long enough, but it was going to take quite a long time. Most likely, she'd drown long before she got hypothermic. *Or the sharks will get you*, she thought, and the hairs stood up on her wet and chilling neck.

Aside from exhaustion and her subsequent drowning, her next greatest enemy was ingesting salt water. She couldn't remember how much she'd have to ingest or in what timeframe, but she knew it would eventually lead to mental dysfunction and organ failure.

She turned her head as another small wave crested beside her. She took the wave in the back of her head mostly, then turned her attention back to staring northwest. Were the kids worried? Was Wyatt looking for her? Surely he was by now, but how would he have any idea that he should look in the middle of the Gulf? The intensity with which she wanted to see his face at that moment was almost more than she could handle. That kind of emotion wasn't going to help her now. In fact, it would weaken her. There was nothing so heavy as despair.

Except perhaps for sodden hiking boots. They had to go. Maggie swung her arms with extra vigor, cupping her hands to move the most water and keep herself afloat, as she pushed at the heel of her left boot with the toe of her right. At first, she thought it was too swollen to come off, and more than once she went under for a few seconds as she struggled to kick off the boot, but the heel of her foot was finally free, and she kicked the boot the rest of the way off.

She treaded water again, catching her breath, and wondered how far that boot was falling. She didn't know for sure how far past the "C" Tower they'd gone, but she knew that the water surrounding the tower was about ninety to a hundred feet. Again, not deep by the standards of the open sea, but deep enough for someone who was treading water. Definitely plenty deep for someone who was terrified of the things that lived beyond the sandbars.

She'd spent at least the first half hour in the water swiveling her head, which didn't help her swim effectively. She'd been looking for a dorsal fin that was cutting the water like birthday cake as it headed straight for her. She finally reminded herself that most sharks attacked from below, and that terrified her more, but it helped her stop looking.

Once she'd taken a few deep breaths, she started digging at her right boot with her naked left foot. Her sock had gone to the bottom with her boot, and she tried to use her toes to gain some kind of purchase on the bent and wrinkled leather of her heel, but she wasn't making any headway, and every ten seconds or so she ended up sinking below the surface.

She was going to have to take the boot off with her hands, and that meant no treading water at all. She was going to have to let herself sink while she worked off the boot. The thought made her want to hit something, and she reached up and slammed her right arm onto the surface.

"I hate you!" she screamed, and it took her a moment to realize she wasn't yelling at the water, or the men who had dumped her into it, or even the sharks. She hated Gregory Boudreaux, who had gifted her with PTSD and robbed her of her natural element.

"I hate you!" she screamed again, with such intensity that her voice broke and she felt like she was throwing up sandpaper.

She'd never voiced that thought before. She wasn't even sure she'd even had the thought before. She'd held her pain at arm's length by regarding him with disdain, disgust, and anger, but she couldn't recall feeling hate.

Now she did. Now, when she needed the Gulf to be her friend again, when she needed to be able to think clearly without her mind being fogged by terror, now she hated Gregory Boudreaux. Now she wanted to resurrect him so that she could choke the life out of him.

She swallowed and found she didn't have enough saliva to soothe her raw throat. When had she last had something to drink? She'd had some coffee right before they'd taken her. Another cup of coffee not too long before that. Four o'clock? Three?

She'd had a big bottle of water with her at work, but she was pretty sure that she'd left half of it on her desk. She'd only been in the Gulf for a little while, but she'd love to have that bottled water now. Exertion, salt water and stress were dehydrating her more quickly than normal.

A small whitecap slapped her in the side of the face, and she wiped the salt water from her eyes, then before she could talk herself into waiting a minute, she took a deep breath and let herself sink below the surface.

She pulled up her knee and grasped at her laces. It was too dark underneath the water for her to see much, and she'd lost her other contact besides. That didn't keep her from swiveling her head left and right as she sank, fully expecting to see all the sharks that had been circling below her. She didn't see them, but she couldn't see more than five feet in any direction. The fact that she couldn't see them made her feel their presence more keenly, and she forced herself to focus on the task at hand before she became too hysterical to do herself any good.

She fumbled with the laces and pulled at the one in her right hand. It was the wrong one, and she was left with a knot. She had sunk at least a dozen feet below the surface, and she struggled back up and took several gulps of air, more from anger than need. Then she took one last breath and dropped below the surface again.

She grasped the boot in both hands and tugged, feeling herself sinking fast. She looked up and saw the lighter shade of dark receding, then quickly looked around her, expecting to see a wide mouth, a jaw full of pain shooting toward her. She saw nothing, but was convinced it was just coming behind her, and she kicked with her leg as she grappled with both hands. She was panicking, and this was making her body consume oxygen too quickly. She felt her chest start to ache, felt her heart begin to pound and her neck swell. Then she felt the boot come free, and she frog-kicked to the surface as the boot twisted away into the deep.

She took a great gasp of air, then another, as the sounds of Alka-Seltzer in her brain faded away and her limbs relaxed.

She had one sock. One of those little no-show socks that she'd actually borrowed from her daughter. She didn't think it was going to make much difference in the prevention of hypothermia, but it was Sky's and she'd hang onto it anyway.

She took another deep breath and started swimming again. Northwest. Always northwest, at least until the last remnants of the sun were gone. She felt like she'd swum long enough and hard enough that she should have come back to the "C" Tower, that if she couldn't see it she should at least be able to hear it, but there was nothing but the sound of water in her ears and the occasional break of a wave.

No more panicking. No more temper tantrums. She needed to reserve all her energy for swimming.

C H A P T E R

NINE

WEDNESDAY, JULY 11TH 8:30 PM

Wyatt walked out of Hole in the Wall Raw Bar, a bright green wooden cottage on Avenue D, a block and a half away from Riverfront Park. Hole in the Wall was busy, its tiny interior filled to a capacity of about forty, but no one in the restaurant had seen Maggie.

He looked up and down the block. There wasn't much else that was open. He'd already been to The Owl, Tamara's and Oyster City Brewing Company. Dwight had gone to Up the Stairs and Apalachicola Coffee was closed. The last Wyatt heard, Dwight was going to check the Soda Fountain. Lon was working Water Street. He had been to Boss Oyster and Café con Leche and was headed down to Up the Creek.

The shops were all closed, even Downtown Books and Purl, which was catty-corner across the street. The streets were all but empty of traffic. Most people who were out had walked to wherever they were.

Wyatt stood looking down the street toward Riverfront Park and rubbed at his face to clear his thoughts. He was about to break down and call his in-laws when his phone buzzed in his back pocket. He pulled it out. He didn't recognize the number.

"Wyatt," he said.

"Wyatt, it's Lon. Any luck?"

"No, not yet. You?"

"Not yet, but I haven't been to Up the Creek yet," Lon answered. "Did you call your boss in on this?"

"No, I tried to get him earlier to see if he sent Maggie out on something, but he didn't answer. In any event, he was in Tallahassee."

"He drives a Chrysler 300, does he not?"

"Yeah. Gray, 2015."

"Well, then he ain't in Tallahassee, 'cause his car's right here."

"Right where?"

"The old city dock, other side of Boudreaux's place."

"I'll be right there."

Wyatt hung up and checked the time on his phone. Half past eight. It was conceivable that Bledsoe had

had a really short meeting with his accountant and then hustled back here, but it wasn't all that likely. It was a ninety-minute drive, not counting whatever traffic there was in Tallahassee.

He started walking toward Riverfront Park, walking down the middle of the street, since nobody else was using it. He was across the street from the park when his phone buzzed again. It was Dwight.

"Hey, Dwight. Anything?"

"Not really." Wyatt could hear him breathing a little heavily, clearly walking. "Gina at the Soda Fountain saw Maggie at Apalachicola Coffee around six or so, when she went to get some of that special lemonade Kirk makes, but I already told you Kirk said she'd been there."

"Yeah." Wyatt had felt a momentary satisfaction that he'd called it—she had been at Kirk's—but that was more than two hours ago and he was less worried then than he was now. She would have called, on someone else's phone or however, but she would have called.

"Dwight, have you heard anything from Bledsoe?"

"Yeah, he calls me at the house all the time," Dwight said.

"Don't be a jerk."

"No, I haven't heard from him."

"You've gotten kind of prickly since you got shot, don't you think?" Wyatt asked, as he crossed the street to the park side and started walking toward Boudreaux's business, the Sea-Fair complex of buildings.

"Reckon it's them taking me off the Percocet," Dwight said.

"Are you in pain or going through withdrawal?"

"Well, yeah I'm in pain, Wyatt. I got shot in my spine," Dwight said. "But I'm not going through withdrawal. I'm just kinda forlorn is all."

Wyatt saw Lon's cruiser up the block. It was parked on the right side of the street. Wyatt could just see the rear end of Bledsoe's car, parked on the other side of a small storage building.

"You know, with Bledsoe out of town, you're the senior officer," Dwight said. "You could call it in, get some more help looking for her."

"He'd have my ass," Wyatt said. "Law enforcement-wise, she's just late for dinner. Besides, he's not out of town."

"He call you back finally?"

"No, but Lon just found his car on Water Street, across from Wefing's. I'm almost there."

"Well, guess I'll head that way, then," Dwight said. "There's no place else to check here."

"I'll see you in a minute," Wyatt said, and disconnected the call as he reached Lon's cruiser. As he did, Lon came walking out of the new bar that Wyatt still thought of as Wefing's Marine, since it had been for a hundred years or so, and still said it was on the side of the building.

"He's not in there," Lon said as he crossed the street. "Only one's been there as early as six-thirty is the bartender, and he hasn't seen Bledsoe *or* Maggie."

"What the hell," Wyatt muttered under his breath as he put his fists on his hips and stared at the back of Bledsoe's car.

"Still can't get him on the phone?" Lon asked as he came to stand beside Wyatt.

"No." He started around the driver's side of the car. "Is it locked?"

"Yeah."

Wyatt felt the hood as he moved around the front. It was cool. He rounded the passenger side and stopped.

On the ground near the car was one of Kirk's to-go cups. He knew it was Kirk's because they were some kind of sustainable, reusable, assembled by virgins in the rainforest kind of cup. He squatted down and picked it up. The lid was askew and the cup dented. Most of the coffee had drained from it, but there was a swallow or two left in the cup, and it was cold but it wasn't bad.

It wasn't a latte, which Maggie drank, but it was Kirk's. Bledsoe drank coffee from the gas station, which was one more reason to make fun of him.

"Whatcha got?" Lon asked behind him.

"Coffee cup from Apalachicola Coffee," Wyatt said. "It's from today, and Maggie was there this evening, but she doesn't drink regular coffee, she drinks lattes."

"Tonight she drinks regular coffee," Dwight piped up behind him.

Wyatt looked over his shoulder.

"Hey, Dwight," Lon said.

"Hey." Dwight looked back at Wyatt. "Kirk said he gave her regular coffee when she was in there."

"Why?" Wyatt stood.

"Just giving her a hard time is all."

Wyatt set the cup down on Bledsoe's hood. His law enforcement side said to keep it. His husband side refused to consider that it might become evidence. But it might.

He looked just down the block at the old brick Crawford building, which had been shuttered for years. "Maybe we need to take a look in there."

"Let's go," Lon said.

They'd taken just a few steps when Wyatt's phone buzzed. It was Lenny again, from dispatch. Wyatt's heart dropped a few inches.

"Wyatt," he said shortly.

"Boss, it's the sheriff. It's bad."

"What?"

"You know Mark Gunderson, runs a couple of shrimp boats out of Eastpoint?"

"No."

"Okay, well, he just called in to the Coast Guard," Lenny said. "They found the sheriff in the water. Said it looks like he got shot in the back."

Wyatt let out a breath he hadn't known he was holding. "Where?"

"I got coordinates."

"I don't know coordinates."

"Okay, well, out near Apalachicola Reef," Lenny said. "It's about ten, twelve miles off the island. Just east of the cut."

"Did this guy see anybody else? A boat?"

"No, uh-uh. He didn't hear anybody shooting, either, but he's running his engines, you know?"

"Yeah. Okay. What's the Coast Guard doing?"

"Well, I talked to Capt. Jessup—you know him, right?"

"Yeah, I do." Jessup had figured in more than one case on the bay during Wyatt's tenure.

"Well, he says they've had some storms down near Steinhatchee, and they've got a few boats in trouble out there, but they're sending an RBS—that's one of their 25-footers—over here to meet up with Mark and take the body, bring it in." Lenny coughed and then went on. "Jessup's on the *Seahawke* from Carrabelle, heading back here."

Wyatt knew the *Seahawke* was an 87-foot Coastal Patrol Boat that Carrabelle, and surrounding areas like Apalach, were lucky to have.

"Can you contact him?"

"Yeah, we can get him on the radio."

"Okay, I need you to tell him that I have reason to think Maggie is wherever Bledsoe was when he got himself killed."

"Oh, crap."

"Then call Skip Shiver, ask him to meet me across from Wefing's. Tell him we need to get search and rescue moving. Then text me those coordinates."

"I'm on it, boss."

Wyatt disconnected the call and stared down at the ground.

"Wyatt?" Dwight spoke quietly.

"Yeah."

"Just 'cause he's dead doesn't mean she is."

"We don't even know for sure she's out there," Lon added.

Wyatt looked over his shoulder. "Bledsoe and Maggie both went missing within a block of each other. He ended up out in the bay. She's out there."

"My cousin Kerry's on search and rescue," Lon said. "I'll call him, give him a heads up."

Lon stepped away and pulled out his phone. Wyatt looked at the coffee cup sitting on the Chrysler's hood. The hood of his dead boss. That part wasn't sinking in yet. But as he stared at the cup, Wyatt had the unbidden thought that Maggie's last cup of coffee simply could not be a plain, old regular coffee.

Then he thought how crazy the thoughts were that popped into a person's head when they were scared.

⚓ ⚓ ⚓

Maggie stared at the last of the sun. She had turned away from Apalach to watch as the sun slipped further and further into the Gulf. Somehow, with all her mental chaos, all her fight or flight response, it had escaped her attention that it would very soon be full-on dark.

It had been such an overcast day, and twilight seemed to last forever in the summer, so that the onset of actual dark came as gradually to her attention as the boiling water did to the frog.

She had abandoned her determined swimming, and been suspended there in that spot, her arms swinging in and out without her asking, her legs pumping slowly, like they were walking up a staircase made of water.

She wasn't sure how long she had been staring at the setting sun. She became aware of her breathing, though, realizing as she did that it had been in the background all along. Short, rasping, loud breaths that made a lot of noise without gathering much oxygen. She swallowed, tried to slow her breathing down, tried to wait longer between breaths, but that seemed to make it worse. She was close to hyperventilating.

She was dangling over the-sea floor, trying to control her breathing, when the sun began to disappear entirely.

"No! No!" she said out loud, and her voice surprised her. It seemed so strange to hear a noise, out there in the vast nothing.

The sun continued sliding beneath the water, like a scoop of ice cream melting into the hot pavement. "No!" Maggie yelled. "No!"

She whipped her head around to face Apalach again. The faint fog of light that hung over her home, which was still hidden behind the horizon, had grown a bit brighter. She stared at it, like she could pick out the one pixel of light that was over her front door or shining from her kitchen window.

She swallowed hard and swiveled her head to look back at the sun, but it wasn't there. Neither was the moon. The faint glimmer on the cresting waves must have been from the memory of light.

She heard an awful noise and didn't know what it was at first; then she realized it was coming from her. It was the sound of her trying to get a breath. She stared hard at the water in front of her, but couldn't penetrate the dark of it at all. She turned around slowly, looking at the surface from every direction. It was just dark, all of it, and now she wouldn't see. She couldn't see them if they came. When they came.

Her entire body below the neck got that tingling sensation that one gets when someone is about to tickle them, that sensation felt as one watched the fingers coming for them. Her entire skin crawled with the knowledge that they were right there. She was mere inches away from feeling the teeth and the ripping. Seconds away from that shock and sur-prise—oh, dear God she hated surprise—seconds away from knowing that the thing she had feared most in the world was actually coming to pass.

She cried out, turned back to face home, and started swimming. Not the effective, natural, focused swimming of her youth, but the panicked, terrified swimming of someone who didn't actually know how to swim. Someone who had found themselves in the deep end well before they were ready.

Some small part of her brain remained rational, and that part screamed at her to stop thrashing. Thrashing that would attract the sharks in the first place, but she couldn't seem to communicate with her arms and legs. They just wanted to go home.

She swam like that for what must have been several minutes, and each second of those minutes she expected to feel the tearing, the crushing, the pulling under and dragging away. Every second was full of abject terror. She'd felt fear before, when facing a man with a gun. She'd felt it trying to survive her flooded yard. She'd felt it back when she was a deputy in uniform, and a crackhead had wrapped his hands around her throat.

But fear and terror were two different things, and she had only felt terror one other time, when she was just a child, staring up at Gregory Boudreaux and the rock he held over his head. Staring at the sky behind him, and wishing she was there. Wishing she was anywhere.

Realizing that she was feeling that same feeling now, that same depth of fear, frightened her even more, and the only thing she could do was try to get away. If she was going to die, she was going to do it one foot closer to her home. Another foot. A yard.

She flailed and kicked, expecting at every micro-second to feel her personal monsters tearing her to shreds of meat.

Her chest seemed to seize up and she heard her breathing change from the shallow, rapid, ragged breaths to deep, gasping moans. She couldn't breathe. She was going to suffocate in the middle of the Gulf. She would suffocate, then sink below, to where her fate waited patiently for her to become a more convenient meal.

Her fingers and feet were crawling with pins and needles, and she felt herself start to sink. Her chin slid below the surface of the slapping water, and she took in a mouthful of salt water, swallowed it before she could plan not to.

Her head went beneath the surface, and she stared at the emptiness of the watery dark, expecting to see that gray, almost mechanical body surging toward her, mouth wide, teeth horrifyingly sharp and plentiful.

As she sank further, she thought for a moment that one of them already had her, that she was being pulled down by the foot and somehow not feeling the pressure or the pain. Small explosions went off in her head, then larger ones. She squeezed her eyes shut, not wanting to see her fears personified. Color and light flickered and burst behind her eyelids, so intense that they almost created sound.

She didn't see her life replayed before her mind's eye, but she did see snapshots, and those snapshots somehow came with sound and smell and taste. Kyle at her breast for the very first time. Wyatt laughing. Daddy running his hand through his hair. Sky doing her makeup in the bathroom, bobby pins sticking out of her mouth. Boudreaux asking her to dance.

At that moment, some functioning part of her brain yelled at her that Death was trying to trick her into drowning because rescue was just minutes away. She saw herself drifting down toward the bottom, head hanging lifelessly, as the hull of a rescue boat slowly passed over her. She saw Wyatt leaning over the side, arm out, ready to grab her the moment he spotted her.

She started to scream, at herself or Wyatt, and took in another mouthful of water. The brine burned her nose, her throat, her chest, and she reached up with her right hand to grab Wyatt's, far above her. Then she reached with her left and kicked. She kicked hard, her chest imploding on itself, and suddenly she was bursting from the water.

Then her mouth opened wide and she drew in the most painful breath of her life.

CHAPTER

TEN

Wyatt wanted ninety seconds alone. Ninety seconds he couldn't spare and wasn't going to get.

He'd called Maggie's parents. Gray, who was with search and rescue anyway, was headed their way. Georgia was on her way to the house to stay with Sky and Kyle, so Amy Shultz could go home and relieve her babysitter. Wyatt had taken the cowardly way out and accepted Georgia's offer to tell the kids. He just wasn't prepared to talk to them without making promises he might break.

A couple of officers from Apalach PD had heard and come by to offer encouragement and support. Two other officers were volunteers with search and rescue, and on their way to the Mill Pond to meet up with their teams. The Mill Pond was at the northern end of Market Street, about half a mile past the end of Water Street. It was where most of the shrimpers and charter guys kept their boats, and Skip Shiver was meeting with the teams there.

The boats went out with at least three people to a vessel. One to man the helm and two to search for their objective, with frequent switches to ward off eye fatigue. Whenever possible, four people were assigned to each boat so that one person at a time could take a break. Staring at the open water for too long tended to make a person see things they weren't looking for.

What Wyatt wanted, besides ninety seconds alone to feel all the crap he was feeling, was to hurry down to the marina, where the SO boat was kept, and get out on the bay, but he knew this wasn't what he needed to do. What he needed to do was finish processing of the scene, since the old dock on Water Street was the last place anyone knew for sure that Maggie and Bledsoe had been.

Lon had broken into Bledsoe's car, and Wyatt was about done going through it. He wore a pair of Latex gloves, as they'd want to print the car, just in case someone they didn't know had been in it or even driven it recently. Maybe Bledsoe hadn't come here of his own volition.

Bledsoe's car was about as informative as a new rental. Manuals, registration and insurance documentation, a free maintenance notebook from Newsome Chrysler in Orlando, which Bledsoe was using faithfully. There was a half-empty water bottle, which Wyatt had given to Deputy Myles Godfrey to process, and a pair of black dress shoes, size eleven, that had been sitting on the back seat.

Bledsoe was a neat freak, or he worshipped his car, or he was just very careful. Bennett Boudreaux had told Maggie once when Bledsoe had first come to the Franklin County SO, that Bledsoe wasn't to be trusted. He hadn't gone into detail, but it was safe to assume he'd known what he was talking about.

Wyatt climbed out of the back seat. As he straightened, he saw Boudreaux himself approaching, hands in the pockets of his impeccably-tailored gray trousers. He sighed. Boudreaux was hard for him to take at any time, but Wyatt really didn't want to deal with him tonight, especially since it concerned Maggie.

"Wyatt," Boudreaux said with a nod.

"Boudreaux," Wyatt said back. He pulled off the gloves.

"May I ask what's going on?" Boudreaux asked. "I was just leaving the office and saw all the commotion."

"Working kind of late, aren't you?" Wyatt asked without caring.

"Yes."

That was all the answer he felt was needed, Wyatt guessed. "We've got a little situation." He hoped that was all the answer that Boudreaux needed.

"Whose car is this?"

Wyatt sighed again and leaned against the trunk, which had held nothing other than a spare tire and a container of leather wipes.

"Sheriff Bledsoe's."

Boudreaux didn't seem surprised. "Why are you looking at it?"

He was going to know soon, anyway, Wyatt figured. He ended up knowing everything, with his connections, but also this was a small town. Everyone who was awake would know by bedtime.

"He's dead," Wyatt answered. He took the clipboard Myles was holding out and signed off on the chain of evidence form.

"Dead in what way?"

"The permanent way," Wyatt said, snapping just a bit.

"I meant by what means?" Boudreaux asked, unruffled.

"Apparently, he was shot. Shrimp boat picked him out of the Gulf."

"When?"

"About half an hour ago."

Boudreaux took a hand from his pocket and ran it through his hair. "Your sheriff left here on a boat around quarter to seven."

Wyatt looked up sharply. "Whose boat?"

"I don't know whose boat it was," Boudreaux answered. "But it was called Lucky Lady, registered in Bradenton. Around thirty feet. I think it might have been a Blackfin. Eighties, I'd say."

"You saw him on the boat?"

"That's what I just said," Boudreaux answered smoothly.

"Was Maggie with him?"

This time Boudreaux blinked a little more rapidly. When he answered, there was a new tension in his voice. "Was she supposed to be with him?"

"No." Wyatt pinched at the bridge of his nose. "She's missing."

"Since when?" Boudreaux asked flatly.

"Since about six-thirty."

"And you have reason to believe she was with Sheriff Bledsoe?"

"Yes, I do."

Boudreaux turned to look back the way he'd come, toward the Gulf. "Is search and rescue going out?"

"Yes. Skip Shiver's coordinating down at the Mill Pond." Wyatt took his cap off and ran a hand over his damp hair. It was after nine and still hot as hell.

Boudreaux pulled his phone from his pocket. "Two missed calls from Shiver. I had my phone off while I was working."

He thumbed through the phone and then dialed a number. "Skip, this is Bennett Boudreaux," he said when Shiver answered. "I'll be there in fifteen minutes. Please tell your people that I'll have the security guard turn on the fuel pump on our dock. Tell them to fill up or top off as they come out Scipio Creek. No charge."

He hung up the phone, and Wyatt squinted at him. "That's awfully generous."

"No, it isn't," Boudreaux replied a bit testily. "The longer they can stay out, the better their chances of finding Maggie."

"You're going out," Wyatt said unnecessarily.

"Of course, I'm going out."

Wyatt watched him as he turned and walked back toward his building.

⚓ ⚓ ⚓

Maggie stopped swimming. Stopped swimming and started thinking.

Every instinct she had told her to swim for shore, even though she had almost no chance of making it. Realistically, she had no chance, but home was the direction she needed to go, and she felt she had a better chance of being spotted by a boat the closer in she got.

The other way was nothing but water, for a very long time, but she needed to stop reacting and start reasoning. She was already becoming exhausted, and she had no way of knowing if she'd made any headway at all. In fact, she was pretty sure she couldn't possibly.

While she wasn't swimming precisely against the current, she was trying to cut across it diagonally. She knew the current ran south-southeast at around two or three knots. Wouldn't she have to swim steadily, without stopping, at a pace of at least four knots, to get any closer to shore?

She didn't trust her memory of physics or her math.

What she did know was that she would quickly become unable to swim, or even tread water, if she kept trying to move against the current. She also knew that if something was caught up in the current from St. George Island, it would eventually end up in…was it Steinhatchee? Suwannee? She tried to picture the charts in her head, tried to remember whether the current was closer to south or closer to southeast. What angle would she be traveling along?

She supposed it didn't matter. She would eventually end up on somebody's shore, somewhere between Steinhatchee and Cedar Key. How long would that take? How many nautical miles was Steinhatchee? Suwannee? She couldn't remember that exactly, either, but her best math said she'd probably wash up somewhere in about thirty-six hours. Or forty-eight.

Regardless of how long it would take, her only chance of making it to land was to go with the current and, to be realistic, she didn't really have a choice. She might be swimming, but she wasn't actually going anywhere. All she was doing was increasing her chance of drowning due to exhaustion.

The idea of actually making the decision to try to float to the opposite coast terrified her. It was insane to think she could stay afloat for as long as that would take. Just the passiveness of it seemed crazy; it went against everything that her emotions thought she should do.

Not too long ago, search and rescue had picked up a fisherman whose boat had been swamped. He'd been in the water for twenty-two hours. Twenty-two hours wasn't going to get her to Steinhatchee or wherever the current was headed. But if he could stay alive for that long, maybe she could, too. And if he could get picked up, maybe she would, too.

Maybe was enough, because it was the best she was going to get. So, she stared to the northwest for a moment, knowing that Wyatt, her kids, her family, were just beyond the horizon. Twenty minutes, on average, would bring a boat from the horizon to her. Everybody who'd ever been on a night watch knew that. She wished she could travel that distance so quickly. Or even at all.

She'd see the other coast before she saw her own, if she managed to survive that long. So Maggie took one last look toward home. Home that was probably still less than a dozen miles away. Then she turned around and faced southeast, faced the eighty or ninety nautical miles of terrifying water that she would have to survive to get back to land.

She didn't know she could still cry; her eyes were so dry and raw. But the tears did come, as she gently treaded the water and felt it carry her away, alone.

WEDNESDAY, JULY 11TH 9:48 PM

Bennett Boudreaux lived in the coveted North
Historic District, a beautiful neighborhood of
meticulously renovated old houses and mature
trees. It boasted Lafayette Park, lifelong residents, and strolls of no more than a few blocks to
get to the bay.

Boudreaux's Low Country-style house on a double
lot wasn't the least bit grandiose, but it was beautiful in its symmetrical simplicity. In the back-yard
that took up the entire second lot, a grove of over a
dozen rare mango trees separated the back porch of
the main house from the cottage that Miss Evangeline and Amelia shared. Boudreaux spent a fortune,
and a good amount of time, growing mangoes much
further north than they liked to be grown. He grew
them for Miss Evangeline.

Boudreaux had changed into khakis, a faded denim shirt, and well-used deck shoes, and he rolled up his shirt cuffs as he walked down the wide steps from the wraparound porch. A brick path lined with tasteful solar lights led from the porch to the front door of the cottage. As he made his way along the path, a breeze kicked up, tousling his hair and setting the leaves of the old mango trees to dancing.

The front door was open, and light spilled out through the screen door and onto the tiny patio. He tapped on the side of the old wooden screen door. He could see Amelia sitting on the wicker couch, watching something on TV. Unlike her mother, Amelia was tall and large-boned, but her skin was the same freckled brown as her mother's, a curious blend of Creole heritage and that of Miss Evangeline's Jamaican father. Back home in Louisiana, where the three of them were from, Amelia, just a few years younger than Boudreaux, had been left with family so that Miss Evangeline could take care of Boudreaux. He often wondered if she resented him for it, but he'd never asked.

Miss Evangeline was nestled into her favorite chair, a brightly-colored afghan across her birdlike legs and her feet propped up on an ottoman. She wore both socks and her house shoes.

Amelia looked up as Boudreaux knocked, and he stepped inside.

"What you doin', Mr. Bennett?" Amelia asked by way of greeting.

"I didn't do nothin' to Mr. Benny, me," her mother barked. "What you go on for?"

"I'm talkin' to Mr. Bennett, Mama," Amelia said as Boudreaux approached, his soles soft against the hardwood floor.

Miss Evangeline looked up from the iPad in her lap as Boudreaux rounded her chair. Her earbuds hung from her ears.

"Hell you do, sneak in the house like them lizard!" she snapped angrily. "Scare me like it again, boy, an' I get up and slap your head right off your neck, me!"

"I apologize," Boudreaux said quietly. "I came back here to let you know that I'll be gone for a while."

"Go where?" Miss Evangeline asked, the thick lenses of her bifocals turning white in the light.

"Search and rescue has been called out," he said.

"You too old to be doin' that anymore," Amelia said. "Let the young men go."

"Where he go?" Miss Evangeline snapped.

"Maggie's missing, out in the Gulf," Boudreaux told Amelia quietly.

"Oh law," she said, almost under her breath. "You goin'?"

"Mutter at me some more, then," Miss Evangeline barked at Amelia. She looked back up at Boudreaux. "Where you go, late like it is?"

"Out with search and rescue," he answered, speaking up. "Maggie is missing. On the water."

Miss Evangeline considered this, sinking back a bit into her chair, though she didn't take her eyes from Boudreaux's. After a moment, she raised a bony arm and pointed toward the screen door.

"Storm come. Look how it do out there," she said. "Ain't no good you go out the water in the storm."

"It's no good for her to be out on the water."

"It ain't no good you go," she said more quietly.

"Did you raise me to let others go out and find her?" he asked gently.

She adjusted her lower denture with her tongue, but she didn't rebut him.

"Will you pray for her?" he asked. "And for me."

"I pray you don't make me pray so much no more, no." Her eyes pooled, and he felt badly about that. "Miss Evangeline gettin' old."

Any other time, he would have made a smart remark. Now, he just felt a gossamer thread of fear winding its way through his gut. She was old, very old. One day she'd be gone, and the other most important person in his life might be dead or dying as they spoke.

"I have to go."

He walked out of the cottage, leaving Miss Evangeline mid-protest behind him. The screen door gently slapped shut, and then all he heard was the panicky leaves and a very distant growl of thunder. His Sig Sauer P226 rubbed against his lower spine, and he adjusted it a bit, pulled his shirttail back over it, then crossed himself as he headed to his car.

⚓ ⚓ ⚓

The Sheriff's Office had a boat that had been confiscated several years before in a drug bust. It was fast but had only one engine and burned fuel like crazy. In any event, speed was the enemy of thoroughness, so Wyatt made his way down to the Mill Pond with everyone else, meeting Axel Blackwell at his slip by prior arrangement.

Axel was a shrimper who'd grown up with Maggie; in fact, they'd been very close, Maggie, Axel, and David. Axel was a serial divorcee and noted local heartthrob, though Wyatt had to wonder why. Axel was good-looking, in that scruffy way some guys were, but his humor was as sharp as a razor and he was a chain-smoker. These didn't seem like the qualities that would attract a woman. Wyatt was rather fond of him, though, partly because he'd shunned MIT to become a shrimper.

Axel's trawler was warming up in one of the front slips, right across from a pavilion where Skip Shiver was holding forth. There were a good twenty-five to thirty people encircling him, and Wyatt headed for the group. When Skip saw him, he raised a hand and people started letting him through.

Skip was a handsome man in his fifties, with a deep tan and a wide smile, both of which could be attributed to his new occupation as a charter captain. Giving tours of the bay and the river made him happy in a way that law enforcement wasn't able to do.

"Hey, Wyatt," Skip said, as Wyatt joined him and a few other guys at the picnic table. "Everyone's got their coordinates and their assigned grids. We have eight boats going out here. We also have six boats going out from Carrabelle and Alligator Point. My counterpart over in Steinhatchee is mobilizing their volunteers to come from that direction."

"Steinhatchee?" Wyatt asked, frowning. "Why from that far?"

"We have to assume that Maggie's in the water, right?" Skip asked. "Why shoot Bledsoe and then keep Maggie hanging around? We're gonna look for this boat, sure, and Coast Guard and law enforcement are looking for it, too, but we have to assume she's in the water. What we're not going to assume is that she's in the same state as Bledsoe. We do that, and we don't look hard enough or long enough for her."

"I agree," Wyatt said.

"Anyway, since we're assuming she's in the water, and alive, we need to look at where she's most likely going." Skip pointed at a laminated navigational chart. "Here's where Sheriff Bledsoe was found. We don't know what time he went in the water, but we do know that the boat went out of Scipio Creek at quarter to seven. It would take a good half hour to an hour, depending on how hard they wanted to run the engines, for them to get to where Bledsoe was found. We can't pinpoint where he went in any better than that at the moment, so we're going to have to use the spot where he was found as our starting location."

"Okay." Wyatt wasn't a boater, and wasn't on the search and rescue team, even when he was sheriff. He appreciated Skip filling him in without making him feel stupid.

"The current through there runs southeast, and it runs between two and three knots. If she went into the water where Bledsoe was found, she'd be about here now," Skip said, pointing at a red circle on the chart. "Her trajectory is going to be this," he added, running his finger in a straight line diagonally across the Gulf. His finger stopped in between Steinhatchee and Crystal River.

It took Wyatt a moment to speak. "Skip, that's almost in Tampa."

Skip nodded at him, and the sympathy on his face made Wyatt turn away, to pretend to care about the car that was pulling into the lot.

"How long would it take for her to—what—make land over there?"

"About forty-eight hours," Skip said kindly.

Wyatt could feel the compassion of the people around them, and it made him feel worse. Now wasn't the time for compassion. Now was the time to find his wife. His very-much-alive wife. And then not let her out of his sight for a very long time. She really had no business being anywhere on her own. They would both stay home, for a very long time. Take all their vacation days and never leave the safety of the back-yard.

Wyatt was yanked back to the moment when Gray stepped up beside him. "Wyatt, you and I both know my girl is tougher than most. God didn't cheat her a bit when He was handing out fortitude."

"You ever pick anybody up, alive, after forty-eight hours?"

Skip piped up behind him. "Forget about timetables for now, Wyatt."

"How am I supposed to do that? Don't you generally have to call it after a certain period of time?"

"The Guard might, but we don't," Skip said firmly.

"Wyatt," Gray said, his voice stern. He waved his hand at the people around them. "She and Axel have been close friends for almost thirty years. She helped deliver Myles's baby in the middle of the ladies' room at The Pig. Duke over there was her softball coach all through junior high and high school."

Gray paused a moment, and Wyatt saw that he was looking at Bennett Boudreaux, who had just come to stand at the edge of the circle. He and Gray regarded each other, Boudreaux nodded an acknowledgment, and Gray nodded back once before looking at Wyatt. "Which one of these people do you think is going to be the first to come back in?"

John Solomon spoke up from the other side of the pavilion. "We'll find her, Wyatt."

"Then we're gonna beat her ass," Axel mumbled from around his cigarette. Wyatt hadn't noticed him leaning against the support column in back.

Wyatt nodded. "Yeah, that's definitely at the top of the to-do list," he said finally, trying to smile.

"Okay, look, Wyatt," Skip said. "Like I said, we don't think about time except where it impacts likely distance traveled, okay? Here's what we need to focus on." He started ticking things off on his fingers, speaking up so everyone could hear. "Maggie's a tiny little thing, and that can work against you as far as keeping warm, but she's got the advantage of summer water temps. That's gonna help her keep her temperature up for a while. What was she wearing last time you saw her?"

Wyatt had to think a moment. Then he saw her at the coffee pot that morning, offering to pick up the cake. "Tan cargo pants and a red t-shirt. She usually has a tank top underneath, too. Boots. Hiking boots."

"Well, if she's thinking straight and physically able, she'll ditch those pretty quick. She's not wearing as much as we'd like, but like I said, water temperature is in our favor right now. I also happen to know that she's a hell of a swimmer. Another plus is that we're about to get some decent rain tonight and tomorrow morning. That's going to provide her with some fresh water."

"She knows enough not to swallow much salt water, too," John said.

"It shuts down your organs, right?" Wyatt asked.

"Not gonna get to that point," Skip said. "Look, Wyatt, she's from—what, Gray? Four generations of oystermen? She's *from* the Gulf, man. It's who she is."

"Was," Wyatt said quietly, looking over at Gray. Gray was well aware of Maggie's phobia about sharks and her long absence from the water.

"Still is," Gray replied. "It's still in there."

Skip got everyone's attention and issued instructions on communicating via SSB, or single-sideband radio. Everyone involved in the operation would be monitoring the same frequency, and everyone would get the same updates and information. Then they got down to who would be on which boats.

Wyatt, Dwight, and Myles would be with Axel on his boat. John Solomon and two fishermen Wyatt didn't know would be with Skip on his. Boudreaux would be taking out one of the shrimp boats in his company's small fleet. Lon and his cousin Kerry were teamed with him. When it came to a fourth, Wyatt was surprised to hear Boudreaux ask for Gray, who owned only an oyster skiff and a small runabout.

Gray looked at Boudreaux a moment, then nodded.

Wyatt and Dwight were several steps behind Axel and Myles as they headed for Axel's boat a few minutes later. Wyatt wanted to run, but he forced himself to accommodate Dwight's pace.

"How many of these you been out on, Dwight?" Wyatt asked him.

Dwight blew out a breath. "First one I went out on was with my grandpa when I was eighteen," he answered. "Reckon there's been about eight or nine."

Wyatt nodded. "That guy Lon mentioned back by Bledsoe's car. The one they found after twenty-four hours?"

"Twenty-two."

"Twenty-two. How'd he survive that long?"

"I couldn't tell you, boss," Dwight said. "Vern Garwood's dumb enough to get run over by a parked car. Reckon if he could make it, Maggie's all set."

CHAPTER

TWELVE

Boudreaux and Gray rode back to Sea-Fair's docks in Boudreaux's black Mercedes. Lon and Kerry followed in Kerry's truck.

They were halfway to Water Street before either one spoke.

"Why'd you want me on your boat?" Gray asked.

It took Boudreaux a moment to answer, and when he did he didn't look at Gray.

"You're the only person I know besides me who won't come back without her."

"Wyatt."

This time Boudreaux did look at Gray, with a half-smile. "Wyatt and I wouldn't last two hours on the same boat."

"Wyatt's a good man," Gray said.

"I like Wyatt," Boudreaux said. "I'm sure he'd rather I didn't, but I do. He has integrity. Character. And he loves Maggie. But he and I will never occupy the same space without tension."

"And you're thinking you and I will?" Gray asked.

"If we must, yes. And we do."

Gray looked out his window as they turned onto the drive that led to the front of the Water Street Hotel & Marina, then curved to become Water Street itself.

"My biggest concern is Maggie's fear of the Gulf," Boudreaux said after a moment.

Gray looked over at him. "She told you about that, did she?"

"No, I saw it for myself. A story for another time. But I saw how she froze in just a few feet of water. She was paralyzed by it."

"Did she tell you why?"

"Yes." Boudreaux sighed quietly. "And I take responsibility for that."

They were quiet again for a moment, as they made their way toward Sea-Fair. There was still a pair of cruisers parked near Bledsoe's car.

"She said she didn't tell me about Gregory Boudreaux because she was afraid I'd kill him and go to jail," Gray said to his window. "I don't know that I would have. It doesn't jibe with my faith. But who's to say?" He looked over at Boudreaux's profile. "Did you kill him?"

Boudreaux stared out his windshield. "Does Maggie think I did?"

"No." Gray waited for more of a response but got none. "Did you?"

Boudreaux looked over at him, his face impassive, then looked back at the road.

"Well, I guess I can appreciate that," Gray said quietly.

⚓   ⚓   ⚓

WEDNESDAY, JULY 11TH 10:42 PM

Wyatt leaned against the port side gunwale, staring out at the dark water that churned past him. Next to him, Axel Blackwell bent his head to light his cigarette. The tip bloomed red, then faded, as he took a deep drag. He looked over at Wyatt.

"Don't wear out your eyes looking for her here," he said. "We're a good six nautical miles from the closest place she could be."

"That's assuming she went in the water around the same time and place as Bledsoe," Wyatt said, raising his voice to be heard over the trawler's twin Cats.

"We don't really have much choice but to assume that, Wyatt," Axel said, blowing out a plume of smoke. "We can't look where she could be, we have to look where she probably is."

Wyatt wasn't sure that was right, when not looking went against every instinct he had, but he knew that Axel and Skip and these other guys, even Boudreaux, knew a whole lot more than he did about the Gulf. He was from Albemarle County, Virginia, a nearly useless onlooker to his own wife's rescue. But he nodded to acknowledge what Axel said and stared out at the water while trying not to actually look at it.

The trawler topped out at nine or ten knots, and Wyatt felt like he was a moment away from jumping overboard and swimming to their assigned grid. It was emotion and irrationality, he knew, but the urge was strong and primal.

"We're moving so damned slow," he couldn't help saying after a minute or so.

"We're moving faster than she is, and that's as fast as we need to go," Axel answered. He stubbed out his cigarette in an old tuna can he kept as an ash-tray. "It was a thing of beauty, back in the old days, watching her swim."

Wyatt stared at Axel for a moment. As far as he knew, Axel didn't know about Maggie's PTSD or the rape that caused it. His best friend, Maggie's former husband, hadn't even known.

"She's kind of on the miniature end of the spectrum, but she had shoulders like a boxer, man," Axel said. "All those days of going out onto the oyster beds with her old man, I guess. We'd go out to the island, or sometimes her folks would take her and David and me over to Destin or Gulf Shores, and we'd just bodysurf for hours. She never got out of the water, man."

Wyatt watched his friend light yet another cigarette. "That was a long time ago, Axel," he said finally. "She doesn't swim anymore."

Axel nodded, squinting against the smoke that rose from his cigarette to his eyes before being taken away on the wind. "I know that. But she's got more salt water in her veins than she does blood." He took a long drag on his cigarette and then blew it out on a gale. "I also know that nothing separates Maggie from her family. If she's got arms and legs, she's keeping her head above water until we get to her."

Maggie heard it again.

It was faint, but it was there: the distant clanging of a bell. The swells had increased to about two-to-three feet, nothing significant in a boat, but pretty detrimental to someone in the water. Maggie found herself in one trough right after the other, with only a moment given her, at the top of a wave, to try to look around.

She had no idea which buoy she might be hearing. She was having trouble with her sense of direction since she'd decided to just go with the current and she and the current both knew which way it was going.

She knew she was headed south-southeast, but she didn't know where she was exactly. She closed her eyes for a second and tried to picture the nav chart. The first thing she remembered was that the notation for the "V" Tower was right in the middle of the compass rose. But the tower wasn't, was it? No, the tower itself was northeast of the notation. No way she'd gone northeast.

The notation for the "SMI" Tower was inside the compass rose, too, but it was way east of where she thought she could be. Surely she hadn't been in the water that long.

She tried to picture "C" Tower on the chart. "C" Tower was the only known that she had. She'd seen it with her own eyes.

The "S" Tower! It was—what?—maybe six, seven miles southeast of "C" Tower? She had no idea how much further south of "C" Tower the boat had gone before she'd gone in the water, but if they'd been only as far as "C" Tower, with the current averaging 2.5 knots, she'd be near "S" Tower in around two-and-a-half, three hours, she thought. But she felt like the current was probably closer to three knots.

She'd gone into the water a little after 7:15. Her beloved old Timex, which had kept on ticking since her high school graduation, had finally stopped at just past eight, but that had been a long time ago. How long had it been dark? Thirty minutes? An hour? It got dark just before nine.

She timed a breath badly and got a load of salt water up her nose and down her throat. She coughed a couple of times, blew her nose into her hand, and she rode back up out of the trough. She whipped her head in the direction from which she thought she'd heard the tower's bell, but she wasn't on the back of the wave long enough. She slid back down, wiped the water from her eyes, and tried to spin as she crested again.

There! She saw the flashing light, she knew she did! She slid back down into the trough, but she knew where to look once she rose back up onto the next wave. It was definitely a tower light.

It took her a few more up-and-down rides to get an idea of how she was moving in relation to the tower's light. The tower's beautiful, tiny white light.

After a few waves, she was able to see that she was definitely being carried south of the "S" Tower, but not by much. Two more waves helped her guess-timate that she would pass a few hundred yards south of it.

She could swim a few hundred yards cross-current. She knew she could because she had to. She wasn't sure she could tread water or float all the way to Steinhatchee or wherever, but she knew for a fact that she could climb up the "S" Tower and hang on until someone found her.

Could she even *get* north of the tower? It was coming up fast. Ten minutes, maybe? The pressure of time, and trying to calculate, made it impossible for her to do so. In a flash of decision, she turned onto her stomach and started pumping, doing her fastest crawl to try to power above the tower in the hopes that once she let go, the current would take her right to it. She knew there had to be a lot more geometry to it, more than she was able to do in her head, but survival was right there where she could see its beacon. She could hold out on that tower for as long as it took for someone to find her.

She took as few breaths as she could, to keep from slowing down even an iota, and she was starting to feel the pinprick sensation of too much exertion versus too little oxygen. Her shoulders and lower back were screaming at her. This was no glassy-surfaced pool, and she couldn't just glide through the water almost effortlessly. Waves constantly broke above her and pushed her down with the weight of their watery mass.

After what felt like several minutes, Maggie stopped long enough to get a few full breaths, put out the fire in her shoulders, and gauge her progress north. She felt something twist inside her when she was able to spot the light, and it looked like she hadn't made any progress at all. The light seemed to be closer, and she thought she could make out the outline of the tower itself, but she was still way too far south of it.

She pushed down the panic that threatened to overwhelm and handicap her and surged forward again. She swam harder than she had ever swum in her life, even back when she and David used to go bodysurfing every day as kids, and they'd race each other out to a promising set. She swam harder than those few times when she'd been caught up in a rip current and had to work herself free of it.

She'd need to be swimming faster than the current to get anywhere at all. How fast was she swimming? How fast *could* she swim? She'd always been an excellent swimmer, but she'd never competed and never been timed. Was she swimming faster than a fast walk? If the burning in her lungs and limbs was any indication, she was swimming at least that fast.

The sudden surge of energy, the adrenaline that started pumping through her veins, reminded her of giving birth to Sky. Active labor had lasted more than eleven hours. When Sky had finally—finally—started moving, Maggie knew that it was five minutes from being over if she just worked hard enough. Then she could finally rest. Then the pain would stop. Then David, who hadn't left her side, could help her to the shower.

She had pushed with a strength she would not ever have believed she possessed. Five pushes and everything in the world was different. Everything was okay. She was okay.

Maggie pumped without stopping, forcing herself not to lift her head to breathe until she absolutely had to. She swam as hard as she could, through five breaths—five pushes— before stopping to see where she was.

At first, she didn't see it, but she could hear it, and it was more clear. A wave slapped over her, pouring water into her ears, and she shook her head so hard it hurt. Once she heard the bell again, she thought she must have gotten turned around somehow, that she must be facing the wrong direction, because it sounded like it was to her left, when it should be to her right.

On the next crest, she looked back the way she was sure she had come, and just managed to see the tiny strobe before she sank back down into a trough. On the next crest, she was able to make out a glint of reflected light somewhere on the metal structure.

She'd passed it. The damn current had carried her past the easternmost marker that she had ever bothered to remember. There were other buoys and towers between her and Steinhatchee, but she couldn't have guessed where any of those might be. Not even with her life depending on it.

THIRTEEN

THURSDAY, JULY 12TH 12:09 AM

Sky sat at the end of the dock that jutted from their back-yard into the bay. She didn't know how long she'd been sitting there, but she supposed it had been a while. The breeze had picked up a few hours ago, and the hair that had been piled on top of her head now blew across her back and into her eyes. The clip had disappeared at some point during the night.

The backs of her thighs hurt from where they'd been pressing into the ends of the planks, and she pulled them up with some difficulty and curled her knees into her chest. Yeah, she'd been there a while, so it must be late. She'd come out there shortly after Grandma had told her and Kyle what was going on.

They'd prayed for her mom and then after a while Kyle had gone to his room and she had come out here. She'd felt badly about leaving Grandma at the kitchen table, staring into her coffee, but she'd wanted some time alone with her thoughts.

In the end, she hadn't thought about much. She'd mostly just stared out at the bay, like she might be able to see her mom from where she sat, if she tried hard enough or wanted it badly enough.

Every now and then, she remembered all of the things that her mom had already survived, all the things that might have done her in, but didn't. Getting shot. The hurricane the year before. Being held hostage by some freak with a vendetta. Mostly she thought about the hurricane, and how proud she'd been of her mother's stamina, her sheer will to get back to her kids and keep them safe.

She was trying to get back to them right now. Sky knew it. She could feel her mother's effort just as plainly as she felt the breeze and the pins and needles in her legs.

She heard the footfalls behind her on the dock, but she didn't turn around. It was only when she saw Kyle's flip-flops beside her that she looked up.

"Hey," she said quietly.

"Hey." Grandma had told him to put on his pajamas earlier, but he was still in his cargo shorts and t-shirt. He didn't have a rebellious bone in his body—yet—so Sky figured he just forgot to obey.

"What are you doing out here?" she asked him.

He gave her a shrug with one shoulder. "Grandma was going to come out and check on you, but I told her I would."

"You want to sit?"

Sky scooted over a bit, and Kyle sat down next to her, his legs dangling off the end of the dock. He was four years younger and small for his age, but he was still the same height as Sky. That wasn't hard. She was an inch shorter than her mom's five-feet-three.

"Where do you think she is?" Kyle asked after a few minutes of silence, both of them staring out into the bay.

It was Sky's turn for an uncommitted shrug. "Out there somewhere."

"She's gotta hate that."

"Yeah."

They were quiet again for a moment.

"I don't want her to be scared," he said after a bit.

"Me, neither," Sky said, but they both knew Mom was terrified if she was alive out there in that water.

"I've been researching survival in the ocean," Kyle said after a while. "Adrift, I mean." Sky didn't say anything, and he went on. "The most important things are for her to conserve her energy and avoid swallowing salt water as much as she can."

"Yeah."

"She has to conserve energy, so she can stay afloat, and so she can keep warm," he went on.

Sky looked over at him. His super-dark hair made his face seem paler than it was. Even in the meager light from the solar lamps at the start of the dock, she could see his long lashes as he slowly blinked out at the water.

Sky had always picked on Kyle a lot, but she adored him. She'd even asked him a couple of years ago if he would be her backup husband. He'd turned red and walked back down the hall to his room without answering.

"Hey," she said to him now. He turned to look at her, his huge green eyes just like their dad's. Man, she wished Dad was here now.

"What?' Kyle asked.

"Remember the hurricane? She came back then, and she'll come back now."

Kyle looked at her for a moment, then turned to look back at the water. "I can't even picture Mom in the water. You know, besides in a pool."

Sky couldn't, either. She had never seen her mom in any water other than a pool. Ever. They knew about Mom's PTSD, and they knew what had caused it. But even though it terrified Maggie to let her kids swim at the beach, she still let them go. She just couldn't go with them. She was afraid that she'd make them afraid and steal the Gulf from them the way someone had stolen it from her.

She couldn't imagine how terrified her mom must be, alone in the dark in the middle of the Gulf, waiting for some shark to come clamp his jaws around her midsection.

She dropped her head onto Kyle's shoulder, then prayed that her mom would come home, and that she would come home sane.

After a moment, she felt Kyle's shoulder move, then felt his hand on her head. She wondered when he had gotten old enough to comfort *her*.

⚓ ⚓ ⚓

The dead man's float went against every single instinct and every phobic synapse in Maggie's brain, but she could not tread water indefinitely. She would wear herself out and then drown.

At first, it had taken her several minutes to stop jerking her head up to look around, or to stop treading water or curling her knees protectively toward her torso. To just hang there, suspended in the water, her face submerged for thirty to sixty seconds at a time, was monumentally challenging. Every time she wanted to lift her face too soon or start paddling, she reminded herself she would die trying to tread water all night. Eventually, it took.

She was unable, however, to force herself to close her eyes to the salt water. She was incapable of dangling there with her eyes closed, so she kept them open, despite the fact that she could see absolutely nothing. It was darker below the surface than it was above it but keeping her eyes open made her feel like she was maintaining some kind of vigilance.

Unfortunately, every time she lifted her head for a breath and opened her eyes to the night air, she realized how much of a toll the water was taking on her eyes. They burned like they were on fire, and she could feel that they were starting to swell. Every blink felt like she was dragging a piece of sandpaper across her eyeballs. She used to swim for hours and hours, never with a mask or goggles. Her eyes had burned by the end of the day, but she couldn't say they'd actually hurt. Were they really so unaccustomed to the salt now?

Every thirty minutes or so, as best as she could judge, she allowed herself to swim slowly for a few minutes. She hated to waste the precious energy, but the exertion warmed her, and the movement made her feel more proactive.

The time she spent just hanging in the water, her eyes open to an underwater world she couldn't see, seemed to drag on forever. The near silence also got to her mentally. That underwater quiet that wasn't so much silence as it was a magnified lack of noise, interrupted only by the pounding of her heart.

She forced herself through it by trying to occupy her mind, by mentally being anywhere but where she was. She didn't choose her thoughts; they seemed to choose themselves. At the moment, her brain had chosen to focus on a day in September, about three years ago. It was a year or so after her divorce, and a year or so before she and Wyatt had gone on their first date. She remembered that it was September because it had been a few days before Daddy's birthday.

It had been a bright, hot day, and Maggie could almost feel the heat of the sun on her face, almost needed to squint against the white light of it.

"I don't think you're actually listening to me," Wyatt said.

"Why do you say that?" Maggie asked, looking up from her tray of raw oysters. They were at Papa Joe's, having a quick lunch before they went around the corner to testify in a parole hearing.

"Because you're not actually listening to me," Wyatt answered. He took a big bite out of his grouper sandwich.

"Yes, I was. You said that you were going to the Dixie theatre tomorrow night with Janice Bell."

Wyatt started to reply, then stuck up a finger as he finished chewing. "Aha! See?" he said once he'd swallowed. "Because that was three topics ago."

"Well, then what were you saying?" Maggie asked. Wyatt's sandwich was half gone and she'd only eaten four of her oysters.

"I said you seemed distant, and I opined that maybe you hadn't gotten much sleep, either."

"I seem distant?"

"Yes."

"That's the part I missed?"

"Yes, because you were too distant to hear me."

"Well, I'm pretty freaking sorry," Maggie said, snapping a bit more than she meant to. "I'm not having my best day."

"You don't have to get all snippy," Wyatt muttered around a French fry.

"I'm not," she said snippily.

"Come on, what's going on?"

Maggie heaved out a sigh and put down the cocktail sauce she'd been holding for no reason.

"Today's my anniversary."

Wyatt sat back. "Yours and David's?" he asked quietly.

"No, mine and Tom Hanks'. Yes, mine and David's."

Wyatt wiped the side of his mouth with a napkin, then put it down. "I'm sorry. Are you okay?"

Maggie could feel the heat of tears threatening, and she blinked them away as she pretended to focus on her oysters.

"Sure," she said. "No."

"You still love him."

Maggie shook her head. "Not the way I did. I care about him. He was my best friend from the time we were twelve." She looked up to find Wyatt watching her, his face blank. "I just…I feel so lost sometimes. So loose, you know, like without an anchor."

Wyatt straightened up. "Look. You were part of a couple pretty much your entire life. It's gonna take some time for you to find your footing on your own."

"I guess."

"You will." He popped a small piece of fish into his mouth. "Why don't you start dating?"

"What?"

"It doesn't have to be anything serious," Wyatt said. "Just find somebody nice to do things with; go places."

Maggie watched him pick at the lettuce that he'd removed from his sandwich.

"I don't think so," Maggie said. "I'm no Janice Bell."

"What's that supposed to mean?"

"I've never even been on a date with anyone other than David," she answered. "I would feel awkward and clunky. And I'm not some stunning creature like Janice."

Wyatt sighed at her, the dimples around his mouth deepening as he frowned. "You're an idiot."

"Why?"

"Because you have no idea—you're completely clueless about how attractive you are. Men stare at you all the time."

"No, they don't."

"Yes, they do. I watch them do it," he said testily. "And who cares if you look like Janice Bell? She's not even my type. I'm just taking her because I want to see the show and she was available."

"Oh, please." Maggie could feel a twinge of something in her gut, and she struggled to identify it.

"What?"

"She's everybody's type."

"She's a friend who happens to be very attractive, yes, but she's not my type." Wyatt was starting to get a little defensive.

"Why not?"

"I need reasons?" Maggie shrugged at him. "She's not the type of person I could imagine just hanging out with on the back porch at night, or staying home to play Cribbage instead of going someplace."

Maggie pictured Wyatt doing those things with someone and felt a little pinch in her stomach. She *didn't like the picture. It made her sad. Was she actually jealous? That would be stupid. Wyatt was her boss, and her friend. Her best friend, now.*

"I'm not interested in dating," Maggie said. "I don't like meeting new people, for one thing. Dating would make my life feel too crowded. I already have all the people I want in it."

She looked up to find Wyatt staring at her, his brows knitted together in a frown.

"Quit looking at me like that," she said. "It's just not for me. But I hope you find the person you're looking for. The back porch person."

"Oh, I will," he said quietly.

Maggie lifted her head and took a slow, deep breath. The bright sunshine was gone. So was the heat, the scent of fried grouper, and the background noise of Papa Joe's. Wyatt was gone, too, and his voice echoed in her water-filled ears. She took another breath, put her face back in the water, and tried to think about playing Cribbage with Wyatt out on the back deck.

⚓ ⚓ ⚓

Amelia came out of her bedroom to use the restroom in the hall. She was surprised to see a dim light coming from the living room, and she walked out there to find her mother sitting in her chair. The small lamp on the table beside her cast a faint circle of light, just enough for Amelia to see by as she made her way across the room. She stopped at Miss Evangeline's chair. The old woman sat there, staring at the far wall, her bony hands folded in her lap.

"Mama, what you doin' sitting out here?" she asked.

Miss Evangeline looked up at her daughter. She didn't have her glasses on; they sat on the table, glinting in the lamplight.

"I wait on Mr. Benny come home," she said.

"You can't just sit here like that, though," Amelia said. "He gonna be out there a long time. That's a big piece of water out there."

"I don't need you to tell me, no," Miss Evangeline replied, looking away. "I wait on the boy come home."

"It's almost one o'clock in the mornin', Mama."

"Girl, I done seen a hunnerd years old," Miss Evangeline snapped. "Don't matter, no, when I sleep and when I be awake. All the same now."

"It's not good for you to be up worryin' like you doin'," Amelia insisted. "It'll make you sick."

"I gon' wait, me." She looked down at her lap. "Go get my maxi-pad for me. I watch the little television till the boy come back."

"He ain't no boy no more, old lady," Amelia said, exasperation creeping into her voice. "He's gonna do what he want to do."

"Who you tellin', 'melia?" Miss Evangeline flicked her lower denture out of and back into place. "I was born knowin' what that boy like."

Miss Evangeline looked down at her hands, at the thousands of tiny clay roads that wound around her hands.

Amelia sighed and walked down the other short hall that led to her mother's bedroom and small bath.

"Born knowin' that boy, me," she heard her mother say behind her.

CHAPTER

FOURTEEN

THURSDAY, JULY 12TH 1:33 AM

Axel had taken over at the helm, and Dwight had come out on deck to take his place on the starboard side. Myles was watching at the stern.

Wyatt was still taking the port side, and he lifted his binoculars and slowly swept from left to right. Dwight had told him to lower the binoculars for a couple of minutes out of every ten, something about eye fatigue, again. Wyatt hadn't paid much attention, but he was trying to do what the more experienced man said.

The wind had picked up, ten to fifteen knots sustained, gusting occasionally to twenty. It wasn't much, but it was coming from the south, so it butted up against the current and caused the small waves to break down upon themselves. Axel had called it confused seas. Dwight called it sloppy water. Whatever it was called, it made Wyatt think he saw Maggie about every three minutes. All that white lining the crests of the waves.

He didn't know why his brain interpreted white as being Maggie, or any other object. He supposed because the whitecaps were a break from the solid, glistening dark. Or maybe he was just so afraid of missing her in the chop that he saw her going down into every trough.

They'd been within their grid for over an hour, and he was getting more frustrated and frightened. He guessed he'd been expecting to see her head bobbing in the water as soon as they'd gotten there but, as usual, Maggie wasn't doing what he expected, or wanted, her to do.

He suddenly remembered a day he hadn't thought about in a long time. It was a few years back. Maggie had been divorced for just a few weeks. They'd been partnering together quite a bit in those days. He'd needed to stay in the game, keep himself on his toes, and they were shorthanded in Criminal Investigations, anyway.

It was in October, Wyatt remembered, because they'd actually had a fairly windy day, with low humidity.

It almost had a tinge of fall to it, and Wyatt missed fall. He loved almost everything about living in Florida, but he missed fall.

They were on their way back to the office when they heard the call that there was a house fire on 6th Street. They were just a few blocks away, and they added their response to that of two Apalach PD cruisers. Dispatch advised that the fire department was on the way.

The house was a small, pale green shotgun cottage. In original condition, not one of the ones that had been remodeled. The house needed paint, but the yard was neat, and there were pots of flowers everywhere. They arrived just after the first Apalach officer, and just before the second.

Mike Hammond was first on scene, and he was talking to an elderly woman who was wearing a pair of blue polyester shorts and a t-shirt with a blue sparkly anchor on it. The woman was crying. Behind her, the little wood house was going up quickly. Maggie and Wyatt hurried toward Mike and the homeowner.

"You don't understand!" the woman was saying. "He's just on the screened porch!"

"Ma'am, I do understand, and I know you want to help him, but we have to wait for the fire department," Mike said.

"What's going on?" Wyatt asked as he and Maggie reached them.

"My cat!" the woman pleaded, staring up at Wyatt.

"Fire broke out in the kitchen. She says a grease fire started in the oven and her fire extinguisher didn't work."

"I just ran out the front after I called you," the woman said. "I couldn't get to the back door."

"Where's the cat?" Maggie asked.

"The screened porch, in back!"

"No," Wyatt said to Maggie. He turned back to the woman. "No one else is in the house?"

"No, I live alone. Well, just me and Norman."

"Norman is your cat?"

"Yes! We were just back there; we heard him meowing," she answered, her voice breaking.

Wyatt looked at Mike. "Paramedics on the way?"

"Yes." They could hear the fire truck's siren approaching. The volunteer fire department was just several blocks away.

"Ma'am, why don't you come sit in my truck?' Wyatt asked. "We'll need the paramedics to check you out, make sure everything's okay."

"I'm fine, I don't need paramedics. I need you to help Norman!"

"Fire department's almost here, ma'am, but we can't go into the house," Wyatt said. "Lt. Redmond can take you over to my truck."

He turned, as did Mike, but Maggie was gone.

"Dammit!" Wyatt barked. He looked over his shoulder at Mike as he jogged around the side of the house. "Take her to my truck."

Wyatt rounded the corner of the little house just as Maggie came out of the screened door to the porch and ran down the three steps. She had a little gray cat in her arms, and the cat was yowling. Behind Maggie, smoke was billowing through the open kitchen window onto the porch and out into the yard.

"What the hell is wrong with you?" Wyatt yelled as Maggie reached the grass.

"He was right there!" Maggie said, as Wyatt pulled her by her elbow toward the front yard. She had to run to keep up with him.

"So's the fire! You—we—but especially you—are not authorized to enter a burning structure!"

"The porch isn't on fire," Maggie said weakly as the cat struggled in her arms.

They reached the side yard, just out of view of the front, as they heard the fire truck pull up to the house. Wyatt jerked Maggie to a stop and turned to face her.

"You do not enter a burning building," he yelled, jabbing a finger toward her chest. He jabbed his finger at the cat. "Especially not for a cat!"

"Why not a cat?"

"Because he is not a human being that we are sworn to protect!" Wyatt yelled. The cat yelled back.

"He counts, Wyatt!" Maggie yelled back.

"Not enough!"

Wyatt stalked away from her, heading for the front yard. He could hear the cat complaining in Maggie's arms as she followed him back out front.

"Norman!" the woman cried as they made the front yard.

She rushed toward them, and Wyatt and Maggie stopped. The firefighters were getting in gear.

"Oh. Norman!" the woman said, taking the cat from Maggie. "I'm so glad you're okay!"

"Your cat seems to be fine," Wyatt said as he walked away. "My deputy's not gonna make it, though."

Wyatt stared out at the choppy water. He had no reason to expect her to be alive, but she almost never did what he expected, which is why he still had some hope.

CHAPTER

FIFTEEN

THURSDAY, JULY 12TH 2:12 AM

Maggie had been thinking.

She was a dark-haired woman in dark water on a dark night. She was going to be very hard to see. So, as she hung limply in the water, she tried to come up with the best plan for improving her visibility.

Her t-shirt was a brick red, not as bright as she would like, but definitely more visible than her dark brown hair. Unfortunately, she really needed it to help delay the onset of hypothermia. She also couldn't figure out how to tie her t-shirt to her head. It had short sleeves.

She had a light blue tank top underneath. Not an ideal color, being in the same section of the color wheel as everything around her, but it wouldn't exactly blend in, either. It was certainly better than dark brown hair.

She wasn't too keen, though, on the idea of taking off both articles of clothing so that she could put the tank top on her head. She thought of pulling the straps out of her sleeves like she did with her bras, but then she'd have to shimmy her legs through the tank, and she wasn't sure she could do that successfully.

She thought about using her blue bra, which she was sure she could affix to her head somehow, but that made her think of Lilo & Stitch, had her picturing Stitch with Noni's bra on his head, and that got her laughing. Laughing because the scene was cute, laughing at the picture of herself being rescued while she wore a bra on her head like a Princess Leia costume gone wrong.

But then she went back to Lilo & Stitch and remembered watching the DVD for the first time with David and Sky, when Sky was just past four. She remembered being curled up in her favorite chair at the old house, Sky on her lap. Sky's hair had smelled of baby shampoo and she'd been transfixed by the movie.

That year for Christmas, David had bought Sky a stuffed Stitch for Christmas. It still sat next to Sky's pillow, in the new house, the house Maggie desperately wanted to go home to. Now. She would smell Sky's hair, feel the boniness of her son as she clutched him, and she would curl up in that same favorite chair, this time with Wyatt, who would be dry and warm and solid.

Maggie wasn't laughing anymore, because home was a long way, and nothing was funny.

She took a break from the Dead Man's float and started treading water again. Her t-shirt would be her best bet for increasing visibility, but should she fasten it to her head somehow now, when there was the least chance of a passing boater or a rescue boat seeing her? Or should she wait until daylight, if she lived that long? What if she put it on now, then lost it, and didn't have it during the day when it would do the most good?

After a few minutes of deliberation, she decided to get the shirt on her head now. What if she was too exhausted to do it in the morning? Or too dead? Even if she didn't make it, she still wanted them to find her.

But how was she going to keep it on her head? The neck was too loose and wide to just pull her shirt up like she was taking it off. It would come off the first time she got hit by a decent wave or went under for some reason. If it had been January, she would have had long sleeves to use as a tie. But if it

had been January, she'd be well on her way to hypothermia by now.

She needed something sharp to cut it with, to cut
a strip of cloth that she could tie around her head,
but she didn't have anything. She had her now-dead
Timex and her belt. She thought the prong of her belt
might be enough to cut a small hole in the fabric,
but she wasn't sure she'd be able to tear the shirt once
she got a hole in it. How was she supposed to tread
water while trying to do that?

But she could probably tear the spaghetti straps
on her tank top and use those like shoelaces, she
thought, and then wished she had the long laces
from the boots she'd discarded. *Stop thinking about
whatever you wish you'd done, Margaret Anne,* she
told herself. *You wish you'd never gone to Riverfront
Park, but that's not helping you much, is it?*

She reached up her left sleeve and pulled on the
strap of her tank top, tugging on it and stretching it
until she got it off her arm. The exertion was more
than she'd expected, trying to keep her head above
water without the use of her right arm, so she rested
a moment before reaching up to do the same with
the strap on her right shoulder. She went under once
before she finally pulled the strap over her wrist,
contorting and bending her hand to pull it through.

She rested a few minutes, taking long, deep breaths. She might have to go under to pull that tank top down over her legs.

After the quick rest, she pulled up her tee shirt, then tugged the tank top down toward her hips. She needed to do as much of this as she could while still above the surface. The tank top was uncooperative when wet, though she doubted it would have been easy to take it off this way under any circumstances. It took quite a few tugs to get it to her hips. Then she rested a bit more.

After a few minutes, she grabbed onto both sides of the tank and pulled them down. She was fine getting it over her butt, but halfway down her thighs she realized she hadn't thought it through. She couldn't keep her head above water without the use of her hands, arms, and legs. Her arms were busy with the tank, and kicking wasn't going to help her get the tank down her legs. She was also afraid she might lose her grip on the tank and drop it.

She was going to have to let herself go underwater to pull it down the rest of the way. She took a few deep, calming breaths, grabbed both sides of the tank again, and let herself drop. She couldn't believe how dark it was underwater. She was certain that things that wanted to surprise and then kill her were just outside her line of sight, which was about two feet in any direction.

She pulled her legs up, curling her knees toward her chest, and pulled. She was just about to explode or take a big swallow of water when she finally got it over her feet. She had sunk about ten feet. She scrambled for the surface, kicking with all her might, gripping the tank tightly in her right hand.

She gasped for air as soon as her face hit the surface, then slowly treaded water as she refilled her lungs and oxygenated her muscles.

It took her several minutes to break the straps on each side. She'd always thought of them as being flimsy and delicate but they actually weren't. Not as delicate as she needed them to be. Finally, she had both straps torn free at the front, and she rested as she pondered the best way to tie the tank onto her head.

The straps weren't long enough, as stretchy as they were, to go completely around her head. She tried several times. Then she laid the tank over her head and pulled the straps under her chin. They reached, with just enough material left to tie a knot. Tying that knot wasn't as simple as it should have been; Maggie's fingers were white, wrinkled and swollen with water.

It wasn't as secure as she would like it to be, but if she was careful she might be able to keep it on there. It might make the difference between being seen and being overlooked, and since a great deal of body heat was lost through the head, maybe it would help her retain some of it. She didn't really have anything to lose by trying. Not if she was being realistic.

She rested a moment, treading water slowly, trying not to work too hard at it. Where was the line between movement to warm the body and energy conservation to preserve that heat? If she'd ever learned the answer, she couldn't remember it now.

She took a couple of slow, deep breaths, let her body go slack, and slid her face back into the water. She opened her eyes, for no reason other than to remind herself that she couldn't see a thing. All around her was darkness, unmarred by moonlight. She could see her arms drifting upward to float along the surface, but she couldn't see anything beyond that. She wondered if that was a blessing. She could feel them circling her just out of sight. Skimming the edges of the personal bubble she pretended she was in. Seconds away from accelerating toward her, mouth wide, teeth stained and broken, ready to save her from drowning.

Axel was back at the helm, and Myles was breaking Wyatt. Wyatt had moved from the starboard side to port and from port to the stern. He'd had regular breaks. He'd had a lot of coffee from Axel's vintage, butter-colored Mr. Coffee. Regardless, he felt the strain of fatigue coming on. Physical fatigue from being up almost twenty-four hours and spending the last several of those staring at every inch of the water that he could. Mental and emotional fatigue from fear, worry, responsibility.

He leaned against the helm station as he drank his fourth or fifth cup of coffee and stared out the port side window.

Almost twelve years now, since Maggie had come into his life. He'd come to Franklin County to accept a job as sheriff, but it wasn't the job that brought him. He made more as a sheriff for Brevard County, and he'd loved living in Cocoa Beach. He'd come to get away from the loss of his first wife, Lily, from the guilt of being unable to protect her from breast cancer, and from the anger he carried, anger toward her, for decisions she had made without him.

Maggie was just one of many people who helped him through those first couple of years. She had been a colleague and a friend, but no more so than anyone else at the SO. Yes, she was beautiful, in a simple and timeless way, but she was married, she was his subordinate, and he was in mourning.

It wasn't until the last year of Maggie's marriage, when the two of them had worked together a great deal in order for her to gain the experience she needed to be promoted to Lieutenant, that he'd realized there was something else there. He'd seen her pain and her vulnerability. He'd seen David's too; they had been friends as well, but Maggie's hurt inspired protective feelings in Wyatt that he hadn't felt in a long time. He reasoned those feelings away. He was just sensitive to women in pain because he carried so much guilt over Lily. He was just a protective male. Nothing more.

But when Maggie's divorce became final a year later, Wyatt realized that it wasn't who or what *he* was; it was who and what *she* was that made him feel the things he did. By that time, they had become best friends. He could tell her anything. Anything but that. For a long time, he hid his love for her behind snarky remarks and beneath his big-brother demeanor.

Now he felt like he was right back where he'd started: fearing for his wife, on the precipice of losing her, and feeling completely helpless to change whatever events loomed just ahead of him.

"Did I ever tell you about the time that Maggie beat somebody up because of me?"

Wyatt turned to look at Axel. He didn't know how Axel could see through a windshield that was covered with a film of tar and nicotine.

"No," he answered, only mildly interested.

Axel lit a new cigarette with the one he was just finishing. "It was our junior year of high school. I'd been going with this girl, Vanessa—"

"I thought your first wife was named—"

"No, I met my first wife in my senior year," Axel interrupted back. "This was another girl. I didn't love her, but I liked her a lot. Lost my virginity with her the summer before."

He stopped for a moment to tap at the glass on one of his gauges. Wyatt took another drink of coffee. He'd seen pictures of Maggie from high school. She'd been a cutie. Actually, when *he* was in high school, he would have called her a fox.

"So, anyway, Vanessa comes to me one day and tells me she's three months pregnant. She hadn't gained an ounce. We hadn't had sex in weeks, but I didn't see any changes." Axel took a long drag of his smoke. "I didn't think I wanted to be attached to this girl the rest of my life, and MIT was already talking to my parents...it was just a bad scene. But after I got done panicking and feeling sorry for myself, I asked her to marry me. My parents flipped their lids. They thought we should just support her financially."

"What did she want?" Wyatt asked when Axel paused.

"Oh, well, she wanted Joey DeVivo. She said 'yes' and everything, and I got her a ring and took her to the doctor appointments and all of that jazz, but a month later, she and her parents came over and told us she'd had a miscarriage in the bathroom."

Axel swallowed hard, and Wyatt waited. He didn't know where Maggie fit into the story, but he cared about the ending because Axel cared about it. Clearly.

"It's weird because I was terrified of having a kid at that age, terrified of being married, and really scared of having to be married to *her*. But when I heard that my kid had died, it just…it just messed me up." He blew out a breath and put out his cigarette, prematurely for him. It was only half-smoked.

"So, about a month later, Maggie was in the girls' locker room, elevating her foot after she twisted it running bases. Some girls, including Vanessa, came in early for soccer. Maggie overheard Vanessa and another girl talking about the fact that the baby hadn't been mine; it had been Joey's, but Joey didn't want it, so she'd said it was mine. After the miscarriage, she dumped me, and they got together. I'd spent two months going through the wringer over a baby that wasn't mine."

"That sucks, Axel," Wyatt said sympathetically.

"Yeah, probably one of the reasons I rushed into it with my first wife. Anyway, Maggie hobbled around the corner and punched Vanessa in the face. Almost knocked her out cold. She got suspended for five days."

"Huh."

"I don't have to tell you that little Mag-Lite is pretty tough when she's pissed, and nothing pisses her off more than someone trying to hurt somebody she loves."

"Agreed."

"Somebody's trying to break her family's hearts, man," Axel said, turning to look at Wyatt. "She's real pissed."

SIXTEEN

THURSDAY, JULY 12TH 2:14 AM

Bennett Boudreaux was on his fifteen-minute break from the helm. Gray was relieving him. Boudreaux leaned against the bulkhead, staring out the port side window, sipping what might likely be the worst coffee he'd ever tasted. He craved his one nightly cigarette, but he'd told himself he wouldn't smoke it until Maggie was found. Or was he telling God? He'd often tried to negotiate with God, though he couldn't say it had ever profited him. God had no need of his offerings.

The SSB squawked to life.

"Team 2 on the *Glory Days,* this is Skip, come in."

It was Skip hailing Axel's boat. A moment later, Axel replied.

"This is Axel with Team 2 on *Glory Days.*"

"Wyatt nearby, Axel?"

"I'm right here, Skip," they heard Wyatt answer.

"Got a message from Terry Coyle." Terry was the other investigator with Maggie's unit. Dwight was about to be the third. "They found your boat's registration. It goes through about three corporations, then ends up being owned by Gulfside Holdings, LLC."

"You know who owns that?" Wyatt asked.

"Yeah, a guy named Gavin Betancourt. Supposedly a mid-level drug dealer over in Tampa."

Boudreaux looked over at Gray, who was looking at him.

"That's right," Wyatt answered. "He was a suspect in a murder case here last year. He's a bad guy, but he wasn't our bad guy. He scooped somebody's deal out from under him, something about distribution in the Panhandle."

"Well, he's the owner of your boat, so I'd say that deal's either gone through or it's still on the table."

"Looks like. Anyone going over there?"

"Tampa PD's on its way," Skip answered. "Just thought I'd let you know. Still no sign of the boat."

"Thanks, Skip," Wyatt said. "Team 2 out."

"Team 1 out," Skip answered, and the radio went silent.

Boudreaux and Gray were quiet for a moment, then Gray spoke.

"This Betancourt. Is he anyone you know?"

Boudreaux looked over at him. "Isn't that a little like asking your black next-door neighbor if he knows Barack Obama?"

Gray didn't answer right away. After a moment, Boudreaux saw the hint of a smile at the corner of his mouth.

"I'd say that's true," Gray finally said.

Boudreaux nodded to no one and went back to looking out the window. It was going to rain soon. He wondered if she was thirsty. He hoped she was thirsty. Only the living knew thirst.

"So, do you know him?" Gray asked.

"No, I do not," Boudreaux answered quietly. "I won't have anything to do with drugs."

"Okay," Gray answered, nodding. "Any thoughts on why he would shoot the sheriff and possibly... hurt...Maggie?"

Boudreaux shook his head slowly. "I know he was trying to partner with some other drug people out of Tallahassee or Gainesville a while back. I know that only because of the case last year."

Gray was quiet for a few minutes. Boudreaux sipped his coffee and looked for Maggie, even though he wasn't supposed to be looking.

"What do you think about the sheriff being killed? Do you think he was investigating these people?"

"No, I think it's more likely that he was working with them."

Gray looked over at him. "Why?"

"Because the governor's a crook who really shouldn't care who the Sheriff of Franklin County is. Why appoint Bledsoe unless he needed him here?"

"Maybe Bledsoe was just a boob that the governor needed out of his way."

"I suppose anything is possible," Boudreaux answered without believing it.

"If Maggie was investigating these drug people, or her boss, I think she would have told Wyatt so," Gray said after a moment.

"Yes."

Boudreaux needed to be back out in the open. He opened the door to the wheelhouse. When he did, a gentle sheet of rain, almost a mist, slid across him.

"Maggie had plans this evening. She wasn't working," Boudreaux said. "I think she was in the wrong place at the wrong time. Happenstance."

Gray turned to face him, looked at him hard. "This is your vessel, Boudreaux, but you should know that I won't be going to back to land without my daughter."

Boudreaux regarded him a moment. "No, you won't," he said quietly.

He stepped out on deck and closed the door behind him. He stood on the side deck, hands on the gunwale, and stared out at the almost-black swells. The foamy crest of their bow wave slipped past him like a white ribbon.

No, they wouldn't be going back without Maggie. And someone had incurred a debt that would not go unpaid.

⚓   ⚓   ⚓

Georgia Redmond stepped out onto the back deck and closed the sliding glass door behind her. On the other side, Stoopid stood staring at his reflection in the glass, murmuring about who knew what. Coco was lying under the kitchen table, keeping cool on the hardwood floor. She'd only eaten half her dinner, and Georgia wondered if she knew somehow.

The rain felt cool and clean on Georgia's face and arms. It was gentle, gliding more than falling, moistening the world rather than actually wetting it. But the breeze was picking up, and Georgia, the wife of an oysterman for forty-one years, knew that stronger weather was coming.

She sat down on the top step of the deck, the wet wood cool and smooth beneath her bare feet, the thin material of her cotton dress quickly becoming damp. Like Maggie, she had always loved the rain. Now Maggie was out in the middle of the Gulf somewhere, either alive and terrified or dead and lost, and every man in her life was out there looking for her. Her coworkers. Her high school friends. Wyatt. Gray. Bennett Boudreaux.

Bennett Boudreaux. He'd liked the rain, too.

It had been in August. 1977. Not quite the heart of hurricane season yet, but they'd been getting a lot of rain. It hadn't dampened the spirits of the locals who were enjoying the Downtown Crawl, an evening of walking from one restaurant, café or pub to another, trying half-price imported beers and new appetizers or desserts at each establishment.

Georgia hadn't attended. She was only eighteen, and not too many eighteen-year-olds in Apalach had money for cocktails and nibbles.

She and Gray had been having some problems, and earlier that week she had told him she thought they needed a little break. He agreed. They'd been together for three years, since their sophomore year in high school. He'd proposed at the beginning of their senior year, and she'd accepted, with her parents' blessing.

But now he was talking about enlisting in the Army or Navy, or possibly going off to college. Georgia knew he wanted to better himself. He was such a smart boy; he read every book he saw, he could quote poetry or

Civil War statistics, and he could create or repair almost anything with his hands. He loved working the oyster beds, the same oyster beds his father, grandfather, and great-grandfather had worked. He even used his grandfather's tongs. But Georgia knew that he thought he should at least try to become someone "better", to accomplish something.

Unfortunately, this left Georgia feeling afraid that he would have to leave her behind to do it, that he would find someone more worldly, more intellectual, more interesting than she. She had become insecure, unsure of herself, and afraid.

That night in August, after talking to Gray down the street at the docks, Georgia had driven over to Riverfront Park, a quiet spot untouched by the noise and cheer just a block away. She'd stood for a while on the dock that lined the front of the park, listening to the shrimp boats creak and groan, crying now and again for a loss that hadn't exactly happened yet.

After a while, she sat down on the half-wall that separated the park from the house next door, watching the river drift by without really seeing it. She didn't hear his footsteps until he was quite close, walking toward her from the other end of the park, near his father's wholesale seafood business.

She knew who he was. Everyone knew who he was by now, though it was his first time in Apalach.

Within just a few weeks, everyone was talking about the handsome, sophisticated, but intimidating Bennett Boudreaux, fresh from Tulane, the antithesis of his father, Albin.

Albin Boudreaux was a big bear of a man, with jet-black hair that was cut very short, and arms like fallen logs. He was disliked by everyone, this Cajun man from Louisiana who had bought the old seafood business and started building it into something.

Now the son was there, too, and he'd made an impression. No one had been comfortable with him, to begin with, with his startling blue eyes that went right through a person, and his quiet standoffishness. People became less comfortable with him when he was confronted by a drunk with a handgun and managed to pin the man's hand to the ground with a nasty-looking switchblade. From what she'd heard, he'd never even raised his voice. Then he calmly wiped the blade with a discarded napkin, put it back in his pocket, and walked away.

Yes, Georgia recognized him, even though she'd only seen him from a distance, the few times she'd seen him at all. He walked toward her quietly, with a certain gracefulness that she found surprising. She waited, and he stopped just a few feet away, his hands in the pockets of his tan trousers. People were right; he did look something like a dark-haired James Dean. He was beautiful, actually.

"I don't want to bother you, but are you all right?"

His voice was smoother than she expected, and his way of speaking much more refined.

"Um, yes," she answered, feeling stupid and childish, though he was only a few years older than she.

"I don't mean to pry," he said, and those blue eyes met hers. They were arresting. "I just saw you sitting out here alone for some time."

She nodded. "I'm okay." She tried a little shrug. "Bad day."

They'd talked for a few minutes, about nothing memorable or significant. Then it had begun to rain, a gentle misting that smelled of good dirt and green grass.

"I have a jacket in my car," he said. "Would you like me to get it for you?"

She shook her head. "No. I don't mind it. I like the rain."

He smiled at her. "So do I."

"But you don't need to stay with me," she said. "I'm sure you have better things to do. Are you on the Downtown Crawl?"

He shook his head. "No, I was working."

They stood there in the cool, quiet rain, talking. Within half an hour, she was telling him all about her problems with Gray, though she did make it sound like they'd broken up for sure. He listened politely, let her talk, and asked questioned that were more kind than prying.

At one point, a tear fell from her right eye, and she hoped that the rain would disguise it, but he'd noticed. He reached over and gently wiped it away with his thumb. Thirty minutes later, she was in his car. An hour later she was in his home—empty with his father away—and losing her virginity.

He was tender and sweet, and she supposed she might have liked it if she hadn't started regretting it almost immediately. But she didn't tell him she'd changed her mind, or that she wanted to leave. She didn't want to go back to feeling like some simple, small-town eighteen-year-old girl, the girl who always did the right thing, the daughter of the Chief of Police.

So she went through with it, pretended she did it all the time, and turned a corner she hadn't even known she was approaching. Her emotions afterward must have been clear, despite her trying to hide them, and he seemed to know that she was sorry.

"You still love your fiancé, don't you?" he asked after they'd gotten dressed.

She nodded, staring at the buttons on her blouse that didn't seem to want to be buttoned. Yes, she did. She hadn't forgotten that tonight, she'd just shoved *it aside, hoping that pretending she was moving on would make it hurt less somehow. Pretending that she was somebody she wasn't; somebody who went home with beautiful men with beautiful eyes. She wasn't, but now she was, wasn't she? It made her sick to her stomach, and she refused Boudreaux's offers of sweet tea or coffee or a meal.*

When he asked if she wanted to leave, she told him she did, and he drove her back to Riverfront Park, to her little red Datsun, to her real life.

He pulled up beside her car and put his own car in park, but he didn't shut off the engine. He looked out his windshield at the park and the river beyond. Then he looked over at her, pinning her with those incredible eyes.

"I'm sorry."

"For what?" she asked.

"I think I took advantage of your breakup," he answered. "In retrospect, in trying to be kind, I wasn't very kind, just opportunistic."

She had a hard time matching his words to his youth and his good look, to his background. Where had he learned to be so elegant at the age of twenty-two or twenty-three?

She reached for the door handle, and he put his hand on her shoulder.

"Georgia," he said softly. "You don't have to take my advice, but I wouldn't tell your boyfriend, whether it's out of spite or guilt. It won't do either one of you any good. Just pretend it never happened, and maybe you'll be able to forget it. You're not a bad person because you were with me."

She nodded, then quickly got out of the car. She didn't look at him again; she just hurried to her car and drove away. Three weeks later he went back to Louisiana without crossing her path again. The week after that, she and Gray got back together.

It was two months after Boudreaux left town that Georgia knew for sure she was pregnant. There was no hiding it from Gray—they'd never been intimate—so she told him the truth. He went away for a couple of weeks, then came back and asked her again to marry him and promised to love her child.

She didn't see Boudreaux again until she was almost five months along. He came back to work with his father, and she and Gray went together to tell him the truth. He advised them that he was Catholic and didn't believe in abortion. They assured him, somewhat indignantly, that abortion was not an option. He assured them that he would take whatever financial responsibility that was necessary, but when they insisted that they wanted nothing from him, that they just wanted to be left alone, he seemed relieved. He *had been polite, almost kind, but clearly grateful that nothing more would come of it. He left soon after, and when his father passed away a year or so later, he came back married, with two stepsons.*

She saw him many times over the years, was even forced to speak to him out of common courtesy now and then. It got easier as the years went along. She loved her husband with every cell in her body, and the guilt of having hurt him so deeply took a long time to recede. Bennett Boudreaux meant nothing to her, meant no more than she had to him, despite his looks and his charm.

But standing now, in the rain that had built from a mist to fat, heavy drops, Georgia thought of him somewhere out there, standing in the rain as he watched for her daughter. Her child. And she was glad he was there.

Her hair had become flattened to her head, clinging to her shoulders like tentacles, but she didn't go inside.

If her baby was out in the rain, then she would be out in the rain, too.

SEVENTEEN

THURSDAY, JULY 12TH 3:52 AM

Skip Shiver had turned his wheel over to Monty Barber, a mullet fisherman that he'd known for years. He grabbed a Coke from the mini-fridge below, then went back up on deck to stand with John Solomon, who was watching off the starboard side. John had put on a navy windbreaker and had the hood pulled up over his head to keep his eyes clear of the rain. Skip wore a light jacket, but he relied on his ball cap to keep his vision clear.

"You doin' all right, John?" Skip asked.

"Good as I can be, my friend," John answered. "What time's it getting to be?"

"Almost four."

"Man, it's just not looking good," John said, shaking his head sadly. "It's just not good."

"It's not good, but it's not over, either," Skip said.

"I know. I know," John said. "I'm not trying to focus on the negative. I just need to get it out now and then."

Skip nodded. "I get it, John." He took a long drink of his Coke. "We just have to remember all of the successful rescue missions, you know what I mean? Lester Carter, those folks from Mississippi, Vern… we've had lots of happy endings."

John rubbed at his close-cropped beard, blond tinged with gray. His slightly round face held none of the cheerfulness for which John was known. John was everybody's friend, five minutes after he met them.

Skip was about to say something when the SSB, installed at the helm, came to life.

"Team 1 on *Gypsy Girl*, this is Wyatt with Team 2 on *Glory Days*, come in."

Skip hurried over to the helm and picked up the handset. "Wyatt, this is Skip. Go ahead."

"Axel says you just advised that Coast Guard's pulling back," Wyatt said. "Is that true?"

Skip could hear the fear and the anger in Wyatt's voice. "No, sir. Just the one plane, and the helicopter that came out from Clearwater's got to refuel."

"Why can't the plane stay out?" Wyatt asked.

"No visibility, Wyatt," Skip answered. "They'll be back out as soon as the weather clears up, which NOAA says is gonna be in about forty-five minutes or so."

There was silence on the other end for a moment. Skip glanced up to find John watching him sympathetically.

"Wyatt?" Skip asked.

"The rain's not all bad," Skip said. "It's water for Maggie."

"Okay, yeah," Wyatt said. "Team 2 out."

"Team 1 out," Skip replied, and replaced the handset.

He popped his Coke can into a cup holder near the helm. "Gimme the wheel back," he said to Monty.

"You sure?" Monty asked, his black brows knitting together. "You still got five minutes."

"I don't need five minutes," Skip said wearily. "I just need to find Maggie Hamilton."

⚓   ⚓   ⚓

Maggie tilted her head back again and opened her mouth wide. It was half-filled with fresh, cool water when a wave slapped against the side of her head, spilling into her mouth and making her choke. She coughed most of it up.

She needed to be smarter about this. She'd only gotten a couple of swallows of pure water since the rain had started. She looked around her. The cloud cover and lack of a moon made it hard to see the waves coming, or even which direction they were coming from. Every now and then, she'd get a glimpse of white froth before a wave curled into itself and went off to be reinvented.

She needed to stop looking and start feeling. She wasn't going to see very many of the waves. She needed to focus on feeling that slight pressure against her, feeling her body being lifted. On the crest, she had a better chance of getting some water into her mouth without also taking in the Gulf.

As she treaded water, trying to get a feel for the movement of the water around her, she tried to remember the math, if she'd ever known it. How many swallows of fresh water did she need to dilute the saltwater she'd ingested? How much salt water did it take to negate the fresh water she took in? She didn't know and bit her lip in frustration. What difference did it make? She was thirsty. If she didn't get at least a minimum of fresh water, her muscles would start cramping and then she'd drown. That's what she knew.

She felt motion, felt herself being pulled upward, and she tilted her head back, waited to feel her body rising, then tilted her head back and opened her mouth. This time, she got enough to swallow before she dropped down again and that or another wave washed over her.

She hadn't wanted to swallow the water right away; she'd wanted to savor it, but her body had snatched it to itself, to meet its own needs, before she could stop it. Even so, it provided a very small bit of relief to her salt-scraped throat.

She waited another bit, missed a couple of waves, then felt herself being lifted again. She tilted her head back, opened her mouth, and then felt herself falling, as a wave she couldn't see curled up behind her and slapped her in the back of the head. The water rushed over her face, filling her nose, her mouth, her eyes.

She coughed and sputtered, righted herself, and before she knew she was going to, she yelled up to the sky, "Are you mad at me?" Her voice was rough and cracked, almost like it wasn't hers at all. "Why are you angry with me?"

Her eyes burned, though she couldn't tell if it was from tears or saltwater. If she was trying to cry, she was out of luck. Her eyes were so dry she had trouble blinking.

She did feel that familiar clamping of the throat, though, the warm sensation at the back of her nose when she was about to cry. Why was she here? She'd prayed a hundred times since she'd fallen in the water; prayed for rescue, for safety, for rescue again. And yet, here she was.

She wasn't perfect by any means, but she had no idea what she might have done, or what collection of things she might have done, to make God put her here. He knew this was the one place she could never, ever be. Why had He let this happen? He was her Father, wasn't He? Wasn't she His child? Had He finally stopped loving her?

"Why am I here?" she yelled, as loudly as she could. The words ripped at her throat as they went out into the night.

She felt her body being lifted, and she tilted her head back and got ready. When she felt like she was high as she was going to get, she opened her mouth and got a decent swallow of fresh water. Then she coasted back down into the trough.

Kirk Lynch made homemade lemonade, from fresh lemons. Not just any lemons, but Meyer lemons, sweet enough to eat like an orange. She thought of that lemonade, and felt her throat constricting, her salivary glands aching in her mouth, trying to produce something. If she made it home, she wanted to have a glass of that lemonade every day for the rest of her life. A gallon. With Wyatt and her babies. She could see the four of them sitting in the metal chairs at Kirk's, glasses covered in condensation, safe, dry, and with all the lemonade they could drink.

She was glad she couldn't cry because she wasn't sure she would ever stop.

"Please don't leave me here," she said quietly.

EIGHTEEN

THURSDAY, JULY 12TH 6:22 AM

Sky woke up in pain. Every muscle seemed to hurt, and her back felt like she'd been folded up in a box all night. She opened her eyes and found herself hunched in the corner of the sectional in the room they called the den. One leg was folded under her and didn't want to move. The other was stretched out, but lying under Kyle, who was curled up on top of her. The last thing she remembered was that they'd sat there, side by side, not talking anymore. Just waiting.

The light through the curtains was a pale pink. Sky got her one leg unfolded, and pins and needles burst into existence, making her wince. She got her foot to the floor anyway and started tapping it back to life. She pulled her other leg out from under Kyle, who sat up like he'd heard a shot.

"What's going on?" he asked.

"Nothing. I'm sorry," Sky said. "Go back to sleep."

"She's not back?"

Sky stood up carefully. "No. Not yet."

"Sky, it's morning."

"I know that!" she said, snapping without meaning to. "I'm sorry. I'm sorry, Kyle."

He nodded. "It's okay. Have you heard from Wyatt?"

"I don't know anything. I just woke up."

She stretched her leg out, tapped it a few more times.

"I'm going to go make some coffee," she said. "Can you go back to sleep?"

Kyle shook his head. "No."

"Okay. Well, let me wake up and I'll fix you something," Sky said. "You never ate last night."

"I'm not hungry. But thanks."

"You need to eat, Kyle."

He shrugged, and she ran a hand along his cheek before walking out into the hall. She used the restroom, then headed for the kitchen. On her way down the hall, past Mom and Wyatt's room, she saw Coco lying at the foot of their bed. Their made bed. Coco raised her head as Sky called her, but she didn't follow. She put her head back down on the quilt, her tags jangling quietly as she did.

Grandma was on the couch in the living room, and it looked like she'd fallen asleep unexpectedly, too. She was slumped in the corner of the couch, her legs curled up beside her. Sky walked over to the couch, unfolded the pale blue afghan that Grandma's mother had made, and laid it over her.

She was sipping her coffee before she realized what was wrong with the house, besides everything. Stoopid wasn't under her feet, or on the counter looking for fallen cereal. Sky took another swallow of coffee and looked out to the back deck. He wasn't there, so they hadn't forgotten him outside.

She walked through the living room and out the front door and found him. He was standing near his rooster door, staring out at the driveway, muttering to no one in particular.

"Hey, Stoopid," she said quietly.

He ruffled his feathers, then settled back down without looking at her. She sat down on the top step of the porch and took another sip of her coffee.

Stoopid tapped closer to the edge of the porch, still staring out at the front yard. He chattered to himself under his breath.

"I don't *know* where she is, dude."

She reached over and rubbed the top of his head with one finger, as he liked to have done. It occurred to her suddenly that he hadn't crowed when the sun started rising. He always did, as soon as it started peeping up from the horizon. She didn't remember him ever forgoing his crow.

She sat there and drank her coffee, holding the hot mug in both hands, letting its warmth seep into her. It was July, and at least eighty degrees already, but she wondered if Mom was cold. A picture flashed into her mind, of her mother drifting with the currents underwater, limbs lifeless, hair floating around her face, and the shock and horror of it made Sky want to gag. She covered it up with a cough, but then she lost control of her own reflexes.

She got up and leaned over the handrail just in time, as her coffee came back up and sprayed into Grandma's yellow roses. After a moment, Sky felt sure she was done and wiped at her mouth. Her legs trembled, though, and she sat back down and tried to pull herself together before she went back inside.

Beside her, Stoopid stared out at the driveway, mumbling to himself.

⚓ ⚓ ⚓

Wyatt had just come out of the head when Skip hailed him on the SSB. He hurried to the wheelhouse as Axel answered.

"Skip, this *Glory Days*. Axel here."

"Axel, is Wyatt at hand?"

"Right here, Skip," Wyatt said loudly. Axel handed him the handset.

"Wyatt, just heard from Tampa PD on the Sat phone. No word on the whereabouts of that boat yet, but they did interview this Gavin Betancourt guy. He says the boat was stolen by some disgruntled former employees a couple of days ago."

"Did he report it?" Wyatt asked.

"No. He says he wanted to give the men a chance to do the right thing."

Wyatt could hear the sarcasm in Skip's voice. "Right. Did he give the names of these disgruntled employees?"

"Yeah, but PD didn't pass them on. Apparently, they're looking for them, though."

"What about Betancourt? Where is he?"

"Oh, he's got an alibi tight as a drum," Skip answered. "He's been at a fundraising event for the Governor in Tallahassee. $2500 a plate. Tons of corroboration."

"That just means he's smart enough to be somewhere conspicuous while his minions do his will."

"Yeah, I'd say so," Skip responded.

"Okay, thanks, Skip," Wyatt said, wearily. "Anything else new?"

"Not since an hour ago, no," Skip answered.

Skip's last report had been that the Coast Guard had nothing new to report.

"Listen, Wyatt, we've got daylight now. That's going to make it much easier for us, okay?"

"Okay."

"Team 1 out."

"Team 2 out," Wyatt responded, and hung up the handset.

Yes, they had daylight now, and it would be easier to spot Maggie in the light of day. But daylight also meant that Maggie would have had to keep herself from drowning all night, assuming she was alive to begin with.

He took off his ball cap and ran his fingers roughly through his hair, trying to wake himself up.

"You all right, man?" Axel asked from the helm.

"Yeah." Wyatt didn't try to make it convincing. He opened the door to the wheelhouse and went back out on deck.

He relieved Dwight, who had been relieving him.

"You hear that?" he asked Dwight.

"Yeah. Did you?"

"What do you mean?"

"It's gonna be a lot easier to see her now," Dwight answered, leaning on his cane.

"Yeah. I heard," Wyatt said. "Go take a break; get off your feet."

Dwight patted him on the shoulder, then hobbled over to the upturned milk crate they'd been using as a break seat.

Wyatt looked out at the water, with its overlay of pinks and oranges, reflections of a sunrise that he hoped Maggie was seeing. He had to believe that she was because if he started thinking she was dead, he might not look as hard for her as he needed to. He could even miss her, and that thought made him sick to his stomach.

CHAPTER
NINETEEN

She'd made it to morning, and it amazed her. Maggie had treaded water as she watched the sun ascend from the horizon and the sky turn from a deep blue to a beautiful display of pink and orange and crimson.

She'd made it to sunrise, but now, several hours later, she was done. Even forcing herself into the Dead Man's Float didn't seem to ease the weariness in her limbs. She'd float for what she guessed was half an hour or so, and then go back to treading water. Then she'd doggy paddle for a while to try to change up the muscles she was using, but all of them were exhausted. Every minute that she stayed afloat was a complete surprise.

She had no earthly idea where she was now. Far. She was far. She didn't know if she was in an area where shrimp boats would be coming in from fishing or charter boats going out. She worked hard to keep her t-shirt on her head, in the hope that some observant boater would happen by and see her.

Nobody was looking for her, she thought, at least not in the Gulf. No one had any reason to think she was out here. They were looking for her, certainly, and she felt a clenching in her chest as she thought about the fear her kids, her parents, Wyatt were going through. But they would be looking for her on land.

Her only chance was for some boat to come by and see her, and so she arranged and rearranged, retied and resituated her makeshift head covering as often as she needed to. Now that the sun was fully up, she'd need the t-shirt to protect her scalp from sunburn, as well.

If she had time to get a sunburn. Every muscle fiber in her body had had enough. She wasn't sure if she had ever felt this level of muscle fatigue; not even when she was giving birth to Sky. Kyle had been easy, as easy a birth as he was a teenager. He'd never been in trouble for anything more than sneaking sweets or cleaning his room by sweeping everything under the bed. Her sweet Kyle. Her Man-Cub.

Please don't let him be too scared, she prayed. *Please take care of my little boy.*

She wasn't going to make it. She rotated her body in a circle, searching for something, anything on the horizon. There was nothing. Granted, her line of sight from the water was much smaller than it would be from a boat, but she still applied the rule: it would take a boat twenty minutes to reach her from the horizon, and right now there was no boat in sight.

Minimum twenty minutes. She had a minimum of twenty minutes to wait for a boat to come by, and her arms and legs, her back and her abs, didn't have twenty minutes left to give her. She was going to drown, out here in the place where she most feared death. All night long, she had worked and prayed to make it to daylight. Now daylight was here, just in time for her to die anyway.

There were patches of golden-brown seaweed all around her. She remembered a book she'd read, or maybe she'd seen a movie, in which a man in a life raft had survived in part by picking up seaweed and shaking everything in it onto the life raft floor. Then he'd snatch up the baby crabs, barnacles, tiny shrimp and anything else that skittered around him. She wasn't hungry, though she felt empty, and she brushed the little bouquets of seaweed aside as she drifted into their paths.

If she was going to drown, she was going to rest until then. She resumed the Dead Man's Float, letting her body hang loose, her face in the water. She was so tired. She was reminded suddenly of another movie. Was it *An Officer and a Gentleman*? Maybe. Maybe some other movie about the military. She was too tired to think. But she vaguely remembered a scene in which a training officer was yelling at a recruit who was treading water in the pool while wearing a backpack.

How did they do that? How did they keep going, carrying all that weight? Did they do it as long as she'd been in the water? She didn't know. She doubted it. She thought she remembered that, in the movie, if the recruit started to fail, other men jumped into the pool to get him. No one was jumping in to get her. There was no one here.

Would Wyatt and the kids know that she had made it this long? If they ever found her body, would they know how hard she had fought to get home to them? Would that help, or would it hurt them more?

Maggie felt the rough scraping of a patch of seaweed grazing her shoulder. She lifted her face to take a breath.

Six inches in front of her, from within another brownish-orange pool of seaweed, Grace Cunningham did the same.

Grace's face was an odd, nauseating shade of bluish-gray, and there were smears of charcoal-gray beneath her closed eyes. Her long, strawberry-blond hair looked thinner than it had in life and seemed to be knitted into the seaweed. Grace didn't open her eyes, but she opened her mouth, with its cracked and swollen lips, and took a loud breath. A breath that sounded like a wind tunnel.

Grace, poor little Grace, who threw herself from the bridge one bright and sunny morning.

Maggie screamed, forgot to float, and went under, swallowing a big gulp of salt water as she did. Her eyes were wide open and she could see Grace's pale-yellow cotton dress billowing around her white legs. She could see small wounds from decay or nibbling fish on Grace's delicate feet as Maggie sank beneath them.

A ray of sunlight hit the water and backlit Grace's body, and Maggie saw her fingers moving, like she was playing the piano or tickling the back of one of her little ones.

Without meaning to, Maggie screamed again. Saltwater rushed into her mouth, but she spit it out and scrambled for the surface. She was going to drown, yes, but she would not be doing it while looking at this horrifying sight.

Her head broke the surface with a splash, and Maggie found herself alone again. A patch of seaweed floated past her, empty of anything but baby shrimp and plastic straws.

Poor, sweet Grace.

"I'm so sorry, Grace!" Maggie yelled hoarsely. "I'm so sorry, baby!"

Then she found out that she could still cry.

CHAPTER

TWENTY

Bennett Boudreaux stared through his binoculars at the water, which had changed from black to gray to a deep blue-green.

"The governor," he heard Gray say behind him. They'd both heard Skip Shiver's conversation with Wyatt earlier.

He looked over his shoulder. "So it seems."

Gray took a sip of coffee from a battered plastic mug, then raised his own binoculars again. "How did you know about the governor?"

It took Boudreaux a moment to phrase an answer he was willing to give. "We share a few acquaintances."

He looked back out at the water. Pretty soon, the sun would get high, and turn the water silver. The light would bounce off the water and into their eyes, making their task more difficult. He had left his sunglasses in his car.

He heard the noise of an engine that didn't sound quite the same as the twin diesels of the trawler. He looked up, and after a moment a Coast Guard plane coasted into view from behind them. It seemed to be going too slowly to remain in the air. He watched it as it continued on a path diagonal to their own. He watched it until he couldn't see it anymore.

If it wasn't going in the wrong direction, he would have hoped that they had Maggie aboard that plane.

"Mr. Boudreaux, time for your break, sir," Lon Woodman said from behind him.

Boudreaux turned to look at Lon. "Okay, thank you."

He handed Lon his binoculars, then got himself a cup of coffee from the wheelhouse and went back out on deck. He leaned against the starboard gunwale, where Gray was stationed. Gray glanced over at him, then back to the water.

"She was supposed to be off today," Gray said to the water. "We were going to have a cookout over at their house." Boudreaux saw his Adam's apple bob as the man swallowed. "My wife made the potato salad last night."

Boudreaux was quiet for a moment. He studied Gray, tall and lanky and seemingly made of sinew. His graying, light-brown hair was long enough to reach his collar in back, to almost cover his eyes in front. The brisk wind blew it across his forehead frequently, and he would reach up and pull it aside.

"I envy you, you know," Boudreaux said quietly.

Gray looked over at him quickly, then put his eyes back to the binoculars. "Why's that?" he asked.

"Well, there's Maggie, of course," Boudreaux answered. "But I envy the simplicity of your life. The serenity of it."

"Nothing too serene about it right now," Gray said with a touch of bitterness.

"No, there isn't," Boudreaux agreed. "Of course, I was speaking in general terms. My impression of your life is that it's clean, spare, uncluttered with the unimportant."

"Are you saying I don't have much to do?"

"I'm saying I think you have a quiet life of your own design."

"And you haven't designed your own life?"

Boudreaux scratched gently at his left eyebrow. "Yes, I certainly did," he answered. "But now and again, I look at the blueprint and it doesn't look as good as it once did."

"There's a lot of things that don't look as good as they did before you got them," Gray said.

"I'm not saying I've regretted everything," Boudreaux said. "We both know I wasn't interested in being Maggie's father."

"Yes, we can agree on that," Gray said.

"It wasn't until Gregory's death, until Maggie handled that case, that I even wanted to know her." He scratched at his brow again. "Even now, I'm not sure I can say that I feel like she's my daughter."

Gray let the binoculars down, rested them on his chest as he looked at Boudreaux.

"She'd better be *something* to you, because you're something to her, and she's had a lot of trouble because of it."

"Of course, she is," Boudreaux said. "She's my friend. My closest friend, I suppose."

Gray nodded curtly.

"I suppose you don't care for that very much," Boudreaux said.

"No, I don't." Gray went back to his binoculars. "But she's a grown woman and she has a right to know you if that's what she wants. And I suppose you have a right, too. That doesn't mean I'll ever like it."

Boudreaux nodded, then took a sip of his coffee and looked out at the water.

Kyle sat at the desk in his bedroom, just next to the open window that looked out onto the back yard. He had four windows open on his computer. One was the survivability model created and used by the Coast Guard, using variables such as clothing worn, time of year, air and water temperatures, physical fitness, body fat ratios and so on to predict a given subject's chances in the water. The Coast Guard used this information to determine, in part, when to stop searching.

The second window was the National Weather Center, where he had checked the temperatures, both in and out of the water, for the last twenty-four hours. A third screen was still open even though he'd finished reading it. It was a story about a woman who had fallen from a cruise ship three years ago and was rescued twenty hours later. The last window open on his monitor was the Excel spreadsheet he'd quickly created to collect and somehow analyze this information.

He was good at researching survival-type stuff, and he knew all the good sources. He loved TV shows on survival, and he had at least a dozen books on survival at sea and on land. It had always fascinated him. Now it meant something. Now he *needed* to know this information.

He looked from his screen up to the window. The palm tree just outside had a pair of cardinals living in it. Mom said there'd been a cardinal couple there as far back as when she was a kid. This had been her room. The bright-red male cardinal, whom he had named He, was flitting from one frond to another, chirping away. The plainer female, whom he'd named She, flew down from somewhere and landed next to her mate. She spread her right wing and dug at something underneath, then smoothed her feathers again.

They looked really happy and—today—Kyle just didn't think that was right.

"Kyle, what are you doing, baby?"

He startled a bit, then turned in his chair to look at Grandma, who leaned in the doorway.

"Hey, Grandma," he said. "Nothing much. Just trying to keep busy."

"You want to come help me make some soup for later?"

He hesitated. "Do you need me to help you?"

His Grandma was still really pretty. Mom looked just like her. It kind of made his chest hurt, seeing her leaning in the doorway like that. Mom did that a lot when they were talking.

She shook her head. "Not really. I just thought it might give you something to do."

"I might come out there in a little bit," he said. "I guess nobody's called?"

"No," she answered gently.

"Wyatt would call right away," Kyle said.

"*Everybody* will call right away."

Kyle nodded. "I'm just gonna finish this project first, if that's okay."

Grandma looked at him for a minute, narrowing her eyes like she was trying to read his mind. Then she shrugged.

"Okay, sweetie," she said. "Let me know if you need anything, okay?"

"I will."

"Where's your sister?"

"She's in the shower." He didn't tell her that he'd heard Sky crying in there, before she turned on Pandora.

"Okay. Well. Come out to the kitchen when you get hungry," Grandma said. "Or if you need company."

"Okay."

He felt bad. Maybe she needed company. But Sky would be out there soon, and he needed to keep researching. He knew that him knowing this stuff wouldn't help anybody else, but he needed to know it. He needed to know what he should be feeling.

He watched Grandma walk on down the hall, then turned back to his computer.

⚓ ⚓ ⚓

Wyatt was the only one among the four people on Axel's boat who didn't actually know how to operate the thing. He'd piloted small runabouts, but nothing this big, nothing with nets and doors and whatnot projecting out of the deck like huge antennae. There was also a decent-looking storm coming, and he wanted no part of that. The trawler was Axel's livelihood, and he didn't want to mess with it. Axel was in complete agreement. Fortunately, Axel was used to staying up for as many as thirty-six hours at a time. Shrimping was hard work.

He watched Axel as he made a note in his ship's log and tried to drink the Gatorade Axel had dug out of a cooler.

Axel had just put down his pencil when Skip came over the SSB.

"This is Skip with Team 1 on *Gypsy Girl*. Wyatt with Team 2 on *Glory Days* come in."

Wyatt jumped up and picked up the handset. "Skip, this is Wyatt on *Glory Days*."

"Hey, Wyatt. Listen, they found your boat, *and* your guys," Skip said. "Caught 'em pulling into the marina in Tampa."

"Who are they?"

"Dead guys, mostly. They opened fire on the officers, and two were DOA at the scene. Noel Chapman is one of the guys, but I forget the other one."

Wyatt's heart started pounding. "What about the third guy? Did they question him?"

"Yeah, he's in rough shape, apparently, but he says Maggie was alive when this Noel guy shoved her overboard. Says she was uninjured. He also says his boss had nothing to do with it, but that's all he's saying. Apparently, he's in surgery now, bullet to the hip. His lawyer's sitting at the hospital waiting."

"But she was unhurt when she went in?"

"That's what he's saying."

Wyatt put the handset to his forehead as he dropped his head and let out a breath. Then he got back on. "Anything else that's news?"

"Just that the guy wasn't sure what time Maggie went in, but it was around quarter-to-eight. They missed a meeting that was supposed to happen at 7:30."

"Did he say why they killed Bledsoe?"

"Apparently he won't cop to that," Skip said. "But that's all I know."

"Okay, thanks, Skip," Wyatt said.

"She's got a good chance, Wyatt," Skip said firmly. "Stay alert."

"We will. Team 2 out."

"Team 1 out."

Wyatt replaced the handset and looked at Axel. "She was alive when she went in."

"That's the theory we've been operating under, yes." Axel squinted at him.

"I couldn't come up with one good reason why she wouldn't have gotten a bullet in the back, too," Wyatt admitted.

Axel nodded. "I get it." He bent his head to light what had to be his three-hundredth cigarette. "Take heart, man. She's too much of a control freak to let somebody else decide where and when she dies, and she damn sure wouldn't pick here and now."

Wyatt had nothing to say. He didn't feel, at that moment, like he could say anything, so he just nodded, opened the door, and went out onto the side deck. Myles was covering his position for another few minutes, so he held onto the gunwale as he made his way toward the bow.

When he reached the bow, he gripped the gunwale with both hands and bent forward at the waist. He took a few deep breaths. He didn't need to be here, feeling sorry for himself or falling apart, but he hadn't realized how heavy the fear was that he'd been carrying all night; the fear that Maggie had been dead before she'd even hit the water. Suddenly, he felt like he'd been holding an anvil over his head all night and had just been permitted to put it down. He wasn't up to analyzing the depth of his relief, but he needed a moment to recover from the good news.

"Boss, you all right?"

Wyatt straightened up. Dwight was standing a few feet away, leaning on his cane, his eyes squinting against the building wind.

"Yeah, I'm okay," Wyatt answered.

"Axel told me the news," Dwight said.

Wyatt nodded, then looked out at the water, where he was supposed to be looking.

"My Grandpa Willard had a saying," Dwight said quietly. "He had a plate in his head, but he was pretty wise. He used to say that sometimes good news will hit you just as hard as the bad."

Wyatt nodded, but he didn't look at Dwight. "It's good news, but we haven't found her yet."

Dwight didn't answer right away. After a moment, Wyatt looked over at him.

"Reckon our chances are a whole lot better than they looked an hour ago," Dwight said.

⚓   ⚓   ⚓

About six nautical miles northwest of Axel's position, Bennett Boudreaux nodded as Gray related the last SSB call. Boudreaux had heard the voices, but he hadn't been able to make out the words. The wind had picked up a good deal, and low, steely clouds were advancing from the east.

He watched Gray walk back to the wheelhouse to take over for Lon. Then he turned and leaned on the port side gunwale.

He felt an enormous wave of relief wash through him; a physical acknowledgment of having been given some kind of reprieve. He'd been afraid—very afraid—that these people had shot Maggie, as they had Bledsoe. The fact that they hadn't didn't guarantee they'd find Maggie alive, but it did improve the odds.

He picked up his binoculars, used his shirttail to wipe the salt from the lenses, and raised them to his eyes.

He was sorry that the man who had physically thrown Maggie overboard was already dead. He knew beyond any doubt that he'd died too easily. But he didn't believe for a moment that Gavin Betancourt had no knowledge of what his men were doing. It was no coincidence that the man was with Governor Troy Spaulding while his men took a meeting that included Spaulding's lap dog.

Betancourt might not have been there, but he would have been the one to call the shots. This shot was going to bring every nightmare he'd ever had directly to his door.

CHAPTER

TWENTY-ONE

THURSDAY, JULY 12TH 1:42 PM

Maggie's sensory memory was excellent. She could recall sounds and smells and tastes so vividly that they became real. She was using that sensory memory to keep her mind off her exhaustion, to force her body to continue on pure, primal instinct. If she thought about her situation, if she thought about swimming or treading water or trying to float, she wouldn't be able to do it anymore.

So she had been challenging herself to remember things in detail; to start with the most general of memories and drill down to every sight and smell and taste she could remember about that moment.

This not only got her mind off her own body for a few minutes, it actually took her out of the water, took her someplace else, where she wasn't dying or scared or cold.

She spent a long time on an evening she'd spent with Boudreaux at his home. She vividly remembered the way the white, floor-length sheers that hung from each side of the open French doors had swished and glided across the hardwood floor. She could see the gleam of moonlight and lamplight reflected in those old, mirror-like floors.

She could hear the music, every note. She even quietly sang the song out loud to herself, as she remembered how it felt to slowly dance across that floor. The barest hint of his elegant cologne as she rested her cheek on his shoulder. The warmth of his hand, resting gently on her back. The sounds of the mango trees whispering outside, gossiping with the wind. The tastes of tequila and lime and salt that lingered on her tongue.

Even though that night had been bittersweet, the memory comforted her now, the way the man always had. She'd been afraid then, and sad. Afraid that he was actually her father. Afraid that he wasn't. Sad that either way, he would no longer be her friend.

The memory didn't seem so comforting after a while, so she moved on to another, the first thing that popped into her mind as she raised her face for a breath. It was Kyle, curled up next to her on the couch. She took her breath and put her face back down in the water.

He was about twelve then, and they were in the old house. They were watching some survival show he loved and that she only watched so she could watch it with him.

It had been cold then, January or February, maybe. She could smell the hot chocolate that was cooling in their mugs on the coffee table. Feel the softness of the blanket he'd grabbed from his bed. See his earnest face as he explained, during a commercial, how educational the show actually was. She smiled, then, underwater, as she saw his hair all out of whack from cuddling on the couch. Heard him tell her, in a voice that hadn't yet started to change, that this stuff might be useful someday.

She lifted her head, almost gasping and taking in water before she did. Her arms and legs starting treading water again. It wasn't An Officer and a Gentleman! It was Kyle's survival show. They'd watched the soldier tread water, the officer training him yelling all the while. Then another man had gotten in the pool and demonstrated how to use a pair of pants as a flotation device.

Maggie could hear her breathing quicken as she tried to remember, to recall the specifics of the illustration. He'd done it a few different ways. Each one started with tying the bottoms of the legs together in a square knot.

In one, he'd blown air into the pants and she'd thought that that one was unlikely to work very easily. Another way was swishing water into the pants, which somehow filled the legs with air rather than water.

Kyle's favorite had been the one where the man held the waistband of the pants and swung them up over his head and then back down into the water in front of him. The pants had just blown right up, and Kyle had thought that was amazing.

She thought about this as she treaded water. She was already getting cold; removing her largest covering didn't seem like a smart thing to do. On the other hand, if she drowned due to exhaustion, it really wouldn't matter how cold she was.

The idea of intentionally going underwater again terrified her. For the last little while—about two or three hours if she was judging the sun's movement correctly—she had realized that she was becoming confused.

Whether it was exhaustion or saltwater or just plain fear, she didn't know, but she was having trouble keeping things straight. Once, she'd caught herself swimming against the current and couldn't remember why or when she'd started doing it. It occurred to her that she might go underwater and forget which way was up. The sky was overcast, almost dark; no bright rays of sunshine reaching down to pull her back to the surface.

She considered this for a moment and decided she wasn't that far gone. She'd only been in the water— how long? Ten hours? Twelve? She looked up at the sky, at the band of marching elephants, gray as an old steel pot, as they made their way west, directly toward her. She wasn't sure she could tread water through this one. The waves were already kicking up, and when that wind from the west met the current that was heading southeast, things would get sloppier.

She made her decision, took a few deep breaths as she unbuttoned her cargo pants, and then ducked underwater. She quickly tugged her pants downward, but as she struggled to get the wet fabric over her wet butt, she saw a dark shape in her peripheral vision. Something darker than the water around her, moving off to her right. She spun to the right, still clutching her pants, but she didn't see anything. She turned right again, but saw nothing there, either.

She was running out of breath. Shadows *might* kill her but drowning definitely would. She pulled at the waistband of her pants, had just gotten them down to her thighs when she saw another movement to her left. Her head swiveled, and she thought she caught a glimpse of something, but she was sinking and her pants were around her knees now and she couldn't kick herself back to the surface that way.

She pulled her knees toward her and pulled the pants down further. Her left foot came free and she was just about to pull the other one out when she felt water—a lot of water—moving above her, from her left to her right.

She instinctively let go of the waistband, spread her arms over her head, and swam for the surface. Her chest was imploding. Something was here. She had no air left, and her pants dangled from her right ankle.

She tried to swim with one leg, keeping her right leg bent in the hope that she wouldn't drop the pants. Then she would have no pants and no flotation device, either. Her heart pounded in her ears, growing more urgent and violent by the beat.

She broke the surface just as she thought she was going to have to breathe, even if she was breathing water.

She gasped for air, deep, throaty breaths, as she tried to stay above water and bring her foot to her hand at the same time.

"Oh, dammit!" she screamed, but it didn't really manage to be a scream. Her throat was raw and swollen, her voice not her own.

She reached down with her left hand and grasped fabric just as she felt the pants drop from her foot. She whipped it up to her and could have cried when her hand came out of the water, holding one leg of her pants.

She rested for a minute, treading water as she tried to recall the video they'd watched. She could. She knew she could.

Tie the hems together in a square knot, tight as you can. Hold the waistband and swing it up over your head and then back down into the water. You can do that. You've given birth without anesthesia. You've won fistfights with meth heads. You dragged an injured Boudreaux across your flooded property. You can flip a pair of pants.

After she felt like she'd gotten enough air to relax and run through the video in her mind's eye enough times, she brought the two pant legs together at the hems. She needed to go up about eight inches to get enough fabric for a good square knot.

As she moved up the fabric, she saw the white and wrinkled and broken skin on her fingers. She'd seen fingers like that before. She looked like a floater, and she wasn't even dead yet.

It took her a few tries to manage the knot. She went down several times while trying, as she just couldn't keep her head above water very long without using her arms. Her fingers felt numb and were clumsily alien to her, but she finally got it. She pulled on the legs as hard as she could. And then grasped the waist of the pants.

She zipped up the zipper, buttoned the button with a great deal of difficulty. She didn't know why they said to do it, but she remembered that they had. Finally, she held the pants as wide open as she could, brought them over her head, and then straight down toward the water. Her unfeeling fingers lost their grip on the left side just before it hit the water, and she took a couple of breaths to calm herself down before she tried again.

She raised the pants as high over her head as she could, and brought them down quickly, before she started to sink. She was amazed, her mouth actually falling open, when the legs of her pants blew up like balloons. She was so surprised that she forgot what she was supposed to do next.

She almost panicked, afraid of losing her precious balloons, but then she remembered. She scrunched the waistband together as tightly as she could with one hand, then pulled the pants over her head, with the knotted legs at the back of her neck. They were surprisingly tight around her neck, like the old life vests that little kids used to wear in the pool. She wrapped her other hand around the bunched fabric of the waist and then tested her handiwork, pushing her neck back against the knot. It seemed sturdy. When she realized that she was actually floating, she started laughing.

She tried to relax against the knot, as building waves started shoving her around, and lightning flashed off to the east. There had been a few small squalls in the last few hours. Unfortunately, the confused seas had slapped her around so frequently and randomly that she had taken in a good deal of saltwater but precious little fresh.

Now, the frequency of the thunderclaps and ominous sky told her that she was in for some weather. She knew the waves would get worse, but if the rainfall was heavy enough, maybe she'd get a decent drink.

She almost didn't care whether she got a drink or not. She was floating and breathing at the same time, and the hardest work she had to do to maintain that was clutch her pants shut as tightly as she could.

TWENTY-TWO

THURSDAY, JULY 12TH 3:12 PM

The rain began pelting the tin roof over the back porch of Bennett Boudreaux's home in earnest. Outside, the mango trees seemed to huddle together for protection, and the bougainvillea were thrashing the side of the little cottage in back.

Miss Evangeline turned away from the kitchen window and scooted her aluminum walker back across the room. The tennis balls on the legs made a soft swishing sound as they moved across the hardwood floor.

She stopped at the stovetop in the middle of the kitchen island and lifted the lid of the soup pot. Steam rose up and fogged her glasses, and she took them off and wiped them on her house-dress.

She bent over the pot and sniffed. The garlic, onions, roux, and seasonings had turned a deep caramel color. She stepped over to the cutting board next to the cooktop, picked up the chef's knife, and with shaky hands, began chopping up a few more cloves of garlic.

Amelia walked into the kitchen from the living room, where she'd been taking a quick nap.

"What the hell you doin' in my kitchen?" she barked.

"You don't cuss me, no," Miss Evangeline said without looking up. "I make the boy some etouffee for come home time."

Amelia came to stand beside her mother. "You crazy-head, you," she said. "You know you don't need to be messin' with knives and stoves."

"I do what I do," Miss Evangeline said indignantly. "I was cookin' before I could eat, me."

"I'll make the etouffee, you want him to have it," Amelia said.

She held out her hand for the knife. Miss Evangeline pointed her bifocal lenses in that direction but didn't move to hand it over.

"He need my etouffee, he do," she said quietly. "Look how the storm do out there. He need more heat. Heat his bones through."

"My etouffee *is* your etouffee, Mama. Where the world you think I learn it?"

Miss Evangeline looked down at the cutting board. "I need the work, me. Busy hands, quiet mind."

"Mama, I'll do it," Amelia said in a kinder tone. "You sit there, and I make you some tea, then you keep me company."

"You say I'm not fit to cook no more, me?" Miss Evangeline's indignation was dimmed somewhat by hurt.

"I'm sayin' you're old enough to have written a book in the Bible, and you didn't have no more than two hours sleep."

Miss Evangeline set the knife down and looked up at Amelia. Tears pooled in her eyes.

"Boy out there the storm. Girl, too. And the juju torment me all the night, it do."

"Juju don't want nothin' to do with Mr. Benny, Mama," Amelia said, tying her apron. "An' it sure as hell don't want to mess with his girl."

⚓ ⚓ ⚓

The rain felt like needles on Maggie's face, but if she dropped her head she wouldn't get any water. The chop had gotten bad, and she was having all she could handle just clenching her pants shut. She'd already had to refill them twice.

The sky directly overhead looked like it was only a few yards away. It was the color of half-burned charcoal and pregnant with rain. Two times out of three, when Maggie tried to get some fresh water in her mouth, she ended up with more sea water. It almost tasted good. At least, it felt good, cooling to her throat. Her tongue was starting to swell a little, and the salt stung it, but the coolness of the water was a relief.

She waited for another swell to lift her and had just opened her mouth when a wave broke over her from behind and she felt herself pushed underwater. She let go of the waistband as she struggled against the force of the water. She was upside down somehow, and swimming the wrong way, then she righted herself. When she broke the surface, her pants were gone, and her tank top was on her back, the straps pulled tightly against her throat.

She pulled the tank top back onto her head and looked around to see if she could find her pants. She spun around in a full circle and didn't see them. She wanted to cry. She wanted to scream. She wanted it to just hurry up and be over.

She struggled to tread water as one wave after another came from one direction after another, slapping her first on one side of the face, and then on the other.

She wanted to go home. She wanted to go home and be with her people. If she could get home, she'd change everything. Why was she out here? Because she wanted to be a cop? She didn't care anymore. It hadn't been worth this. She wanted to go home and work a register at CVS or clean rooms at the Water Street Hotel. She'd been selfish to choose the profession she had.

Another wave slapped her right in the face, and she reached up to wipe her eyes as she felt herself being pulled up the face of another. As she reached the crest, she saw him, just a few yards away. She knew that black hair, she knew the shape of that face as he turned partly toward her, like he might look over his shoulder.

"Kyle!" she screamed, only barely. He was swimming away from her, swimming easily, as though the water was as still as a swimming pool, but the only thing worse than Maggie being out here was Kyle being out here.

"Kyle!" she yelled again, her voice breaking, and seeming to blow away behind her.

He turned then, and she almost forgot to tread water. It wasn't Kyle. It was David. Her sweet twelve or thirteen-year-old David, smiling widely like he was having fun. He held up a hand and she saw a glint of metal, metal with a light at the top, like a flashlight. He flicked it on and off at her, then smiled.

"What's wrong with you?" he called just loud enough for her to hear. "Quit swimming like such a girl."

"David?"

"Come on!" he said, and turned away again, started stroking smoothly, and went further away.

"David, wait!" Maggie's throat seized as she yelled; it seemed like the entire length of her throat was cracking apart.

The rain began to slow, its pelting of her head and face less painful, but she hardly noticed. She didn't want to take her eyes off of David, but she could swim faster if she did the crawl, and she put her head down and started stroking. After ten or so strokes, she lifted her head.

"Don't be such a wimp," he called to her. He held the flashlight up as high as he could, like she was supposed to come get it. Then he turned around and started swimming again, as a weak ray of sunlight peeked through the clouds overhead.

"David, wait!"

Maggie started swimming again, swimming hard. She swam with her eyes open, hoping she would see his legs just in front of her. A bit more of the sun shone through the clouds, and she could see at least five or six feet ahead, but he wasn't there.

She lifted her head again, took a deep breath. She couldn't see David, but she could see the light he was holding, so he wasn't too far ahead. The light was weaker, dulled by the growing sunlight, but it was still there.

"David!" she called.

Just then, a swell lifted her up, and she saw. Not David. Not David's flashlight, but the light at the top of a buoy, one of the triangular metal buoys that she'd called lighthouses when she was a child. It was no more than a hundred yards ahead.

She took a deep breath and started swimming, swimming harder, possibly, than she ever had. It had to be real. It had to be, or else she was wasting the last of what she had in her.

She swam without a breath as long as she could, her shoulders and abs burning with the effort. When she finally stopped to take a breath, she swore she was closer. Not close, but closer.

"Oh. Oh, God, please," she said quietly.

Just then she felt a bump on her left hip, and she cried out. She looked around but saw nothing except the blue-green waves, and the light of the buoy, so far away it now seemed. She didn't know how her heart could speed up and simultaneously stop altogether, but that was what she felt. Her breathing became short and jagged, and her face began to tingle.

She seemed to feel the movement of the current underwater before she felt the rubbing against her left calf. It was like rubbery sandpaper, and it seemed to graze her leg forever as it moved past her.

Maggie opened her mouth but made no sound. She had no breath left to scream.

CHAPTER

TWENTY-THREE

Wyatt looked over Axel's shoulder as he consulted the electronic chart displayed on the iPad that sat in a holder just above the helm.

"What are you looking at?" he asked.

"Our turnaround point," Axel answered.

"Turnaround?" Wyatt snapped.

"Wyatt, this baby's got some serious fuel tanks, but we've been running at our max of nine knots for fifteen hours. That's fifteen hours to get back. "

"She could be right ahead," Wyatt said, feeling panic rise up in his chest. He'd get out and swim if he needed to, but he wasn't going back without Maggie.

"She could be right behind us, too, and we missed her," Axel said. "Listen, the team from Steinhatchee has it as their turnaround, too. We're not leaving any blanks unfilled, Wyatt."

Wyatt swallowed hard and looked at the chart. "So where are we turning around then?"

"Here," Axel answered, pointing at a spot on the chart just past some icon Wyatt didn't know.

"What's this thing?" Wyatt pointed at the symbol.

"C-14 buoy. We turn one nautical mile beyond it. They turn around one nautical beyond it on this side."

"Okay."

"Storms are gone for now, so visibility is better," Axel said. "We might see her on the way back, where we missed her before. Hang in there, man."

⚓ ⚓ ⚓

Sky was scrubbing the tub shower that she and Kyle shared for the third time. She'd finished off one can of Comet and was working on another. Her knees hurt, despite the fact that she was kneeling on the blue and white striped bath rug she'd just washed.

A stubborn stain, rust in the shape of a bobby pin she'd dropped and left there for a week, was giving her a hard time. She'd worn all the roughness off the scrubber sponge, and she tossed it in the trash can and pulled another one out of the blue plastic tote.

A lock of hair slipped from underneath the bandana she'd tied around her head. Irritated, she tucked it in and got back to scrubbing.

Mom had been asking her for two weeks to clean their bathroom. She and Kyle alternated weeks because neither one of them liked the job, but she hadn't been able to talk Kyle into taking her turn. It wasn't like Mom was asking so much; she worked hard, and she really didn't give them that many chores. She was too much of a control freak, and, Sky knew, a little too easy on her kids.

Now Mom was going through this ordeal, and when she got back she'd be tired and—Sky just needed to get it clean. It was just one bathroom. Not too much to require from somebody who was about to leave for college.

She looked through the tote and found some creamy cleanser. She squeezed it out on top of the grainy blue Comet and went back to scrubbing.

Mom didn't want her to leave; Sky knew she didn't. Well, that wasn't totally accurate. Mom wanted her to leave, she just didn't want her to have to go so far. She was proud of Sky's scholarship to Florida State, her own alma mater, but if Sky had said she was going to live at home and commute to some community college in Panama City, she knew her Mom would have cried with relief.

She wanted Sky to do her best, have the best, achieve the most. Sky knew that. But she also felt like time was running out for the two of them to spend time together.

Sky swiped at the pale blue muck with her hand. The freaking rust was still there! She dumped another blob of creamy cleanser on it, turned the scrubby around to the mostly unused edge, and started scrubbing even harder.

Sky had been so excited about graduating, so anxious to go off to college and experience new things, meet new people. At the same time, she'd wanted to spend time with friends who were staying in Apalach or going to other colleges. There'd been lots of picnics and going-away parties and beach barbecues. Meanwhile, Mom sat home wishing she had a little more time.

Sky turned the water on and splashed some over the cleanser. The bobby pin-shaped stain was intact.

Sky jumped up. "Dammit!" she yelled. She picked up the tote of cleaning supplies and threw it up against the shower wall. "Dammit!" she yelled, even louder.

The bathroom door flew open, and Grandma stared at her in surprise.

Sky stood there on the blue and white striped rug, sponges, cleaners, and Clorox wipes scattered around her feet.

"Baby, what's going on?" Grandma asked.

"I can't even get the rust stain out!" Sky yelled, and she felt something break inside her.

⚓ ⚓ ⚓

Maggie tried to breathe. She tried not to let herself actually die from fear, as she slowly turned in a circle, her arms waving just below the surface, her eyes raking the water around her. She couldn't see it. She didn't know where it was. It had gone behind her. She looked for fins, for ripples, for some movement of water that didn't belong, but she saw nothing, just the blinking light of the buoy that now seemed tragically far away.

She was going to make it. She *could* have made it. Why did it wait until she could see her own survival right in front of her? Why did God even let her see the buoy? It would have been kinder if the end had come when she was convinced it was coming anyway. Now she had to lose the hope that she had just been given. Beneath the terror she felt lay a sadness so profound that it made her ache.

She wanted to circle around again, but she was afraid to move more than she already was to stay afloat. They were attracted to movement, she knew. Was it better to try to be still? Would she be better off in the Dead Man's Float again, dangling like bait from a hook?

She was surprised to feel a tear falling down her left cheek.

She swallowed hard. She'd read an awful lot about sharks, her terror drawing her to the very thing she feared. One of the things she'd read was that the best way to repel a shark was to face it; that they preferred sneak attacks from below or behind and saw confrontation as a sign of aggression from something that must not be prey.

She didn't know if that was true, but what if it was? She had no other defense. The idea of watching the shark come for her, of seeing it come in for the kill, made her feel like her mind was going to come apart. But she was terrified of surprises; she had been since the day over twenty years ago when Gregory Boudreaux had surprised her in the woods.

If this shark was going to kill her, he was going to kill her. At least all of this would finally be over. And if she had to see him coming, if she had to watch him take her head in his jaws, well, at least he hadn't surprised her.

She sensed movement behind her, felt every inch of skin tingle. Now. She would do it now.

She didn't bother taking a breath; she just turned around and then let herself sink below the surface.

At first, she saw nothing, but then, ten yards or so ahead, she saw a shape taking form. Movement from side to side. And then there he was.

It was at least six feet long; not at all huge by shark standards, but as big as the Empire State Building to her. Her heart was slamming in her ears and every inch of her body was vibrating as she hung suspended there, neither sinking nor rising.

She was aware of her own amazement, that the thing she'd feared for so long was actually coming to pass. She'd stayed out of the water for twenty-three years so that this could never, ever happen, and yet here she was.

She watched as it swam toward her, its tail swinging from side to side in an almost graceful motion, and she said her goodbyes without words. She had no words, only hope that her people would be okay.

The shark got within three feet of her, and she waited, eyes open. Then it veered just a touch to her right, and as it passed within a foot of her, she stared into its right eye, and its right eye stared into both of hers.

The eye was black, and flat somehow. Lacking in something she saw in the eyes of a cat, a person, her rooster, her dog. And yet, it didn't look as malevolent, as evil as it had on *Shark Week* or in her imagination. It wasn't warm, but it wasn't full of primal hate, either.

Then it was past her, its tail close enough for her face to feel the current of water it pushed her way. She slowly turned to look after it, to wait for it to come back and get her from behind, but it kept swimming,

She watched as long as she could but saw no further sign of it. She swam to the surface as calmly as she could, trying not to thrash provocatively. She took two slow, deep breaths of air, then went beneath the surface again. She turned two full circles and saw nothing.

She came back to the surface, took one more look around, and started swimming toward the buoy. Let it surprise her. She might have a chance, and she was taking it. She swam as smoothly as she could, but she swam hard and fast, with an energy reserve she would not have believed existed just a few minutes ago.

She lifted her face for a breath only when she absolutely had to, and on her sixth breath, she looked up and it was there. The buoy. It startled her so much that it took her a second to reach out to it.

The base was about ten feet around. She grabbed onto it with one hand, then reached up for one of the red-painted metal bars the crisscrossed its side.

She felt a sharp, scraping pain, and jerked her hand back. There were several small cuts on her hand, and tiny bits of red-painted metal buried in the white, puffy flesh. Blood dripped from a few of the cuts, and she thought about the fact that every shark in a ten-mile radius was going to come looking for her. She didn't care. If one of them wanted her, it was going to have to climb up there and get her, because she was getting out of the water *now*.

She took a deep breath, grabbed onto the bar again and pulled. She threw one leg up onto the base, wincing as she felt loose shards of metal and crusty barnacles scraping at her. She pressed her swollen lips together firmly and then dragged the rest of herself onto the buoy.

She fell face down on the buoy's base, surprised to find that her little blue tank top was still attached to her head. She felt it now, wet against the back of her neck.

The base was cool and rough beneath her cheek. She carefully put both palms flat against the surface, daring it to disappear beneath her fingers, but it didn't. When she lifted her right hand, there were several spots of blood left behind.

She closed her eyes in gratitude and weariness. When she opened them, David was there, her grown husband David, his elbows resting on top of the buoy's base as he smiled at her. His close-cropped beard shimmered in the sunlight, and his smile was kind.

"You look tired, babe," he said, and it was his voice; the voice she remembered so well.

She looked right into his green eyes. "David, are you real?" she whispered.

He tilted his head just a bit and reached out to touch her face. She couldn't feel it.

"No, babe," he said gently. "But I wish I was."

CHAPTER
TWENTY-FOUR

The sun was in his eyes as Wyatt stared through the binoculars on the starboard side of the trawler. The rays glinted and sparkled on the water, making him see things that weren't there. They were about to turn around, so he was already looking where they'd been, looking where they were about to go again.

"There!" Dwight yelled behind him from his post on the port side. "There!"

Wyatt turned around, his heart pounding. Dwight was pointing off the port side, and at first, he was blocking Wyatt's view of what he was pointing at.

But then he turned to look over his shoulder at Wyatt, and Wyatt saw. He saw a big red thing bobbing gently in the water, and he saw his wife lying on it in her underwear and a tee shirt, her face turned toward him, her eyes closed.

He dropped the binoculars, took two long strides, and stepped onto the gunwale, then dove over the side. Just before he hit the water, he heard Dwight yell at Axel to come about. Then he was in the water, swimming the fifty or so yards to the buoy.

He reached it faster than he would have thought possible. "Maggie!"

She didn't answer. Her eyelids didn't move. He grabbed a crossbar and pulled himself out of the water. Then he knelt beside her and gently rolled her onto her back. Her face was sunburned, her lips horribly swollen and cracked. Her eyes, too, were swollen, as though she'd been stung by bees, to which she was allergic.

"Maggie!"

He heard the rumbling of the trawler as it turned toward the buoy. He vaguely heard Dwight yelling at him.

Maggie's eyelids twitched, and then she opened them, but only partway. They looked odd. Different. But her eyes were open.

"Wyatt," she whispered hoarsely. "Are you really here?"

"Yes," he said, his voice breaking as he gathered her into his chest.

"I need you to be here," she said against his shirt.

"I am."

⚓   ⚓   ⚓

Just a few minutes later, Wyatt and Maggie climbed into the dinghy, then Axel and Myles pulled the attached line, grasping hand over hand until the dinghy was alongside the trawler. They secured it to the nearest cleats, then pulled first Maggie and then Wyatt aboard. Axel couldn't believe he was looking *at* Maggie, after twenty-some hours of looking *for* her.

She had lost her pants somehow, and she had some blue thing tied to her head, but she was alive.

She couldn't stand; Wyatt sat down on the deck of the boat and pulled her into his lap as Dwight handed Axel a blanket. Axel held it out to Wyatt as Maggie opened her eyes and looked at him.

"Well, hey there, Linus," Axel said with a grin. "You need a ride to the Christmas pageant?

⚓   ⚓   ⚓

Six nautical miles away, Gray and Boudreaux heard Dwight yelling over the SSB. Maggie had been found and found alive. A Coast Guard helicopter was on its way to pick up Maggie and Wyatt and transport them to the nearest hospital with a helipad, which was in Perry.

Gray leaned through the back window of the wheelhouse. "Can I call my family on that thing?" he yelled. "I need to call my family."

Boudreaux leaned back against the port side gunwale and let out a long breath. Then he crossed himself and kissed his fist.

TWENTY-FIVE

The next day, just after four, the Coast Guard helicopter brought Maggie and Wyatt home, as a
courtesy from one branch of law enforcement
to another. The ride only took forty-five minutes
or so, and the helicopter landed in the parking lot
of Weems Memorial.

One of the Coast Guard handed Maggie down
from the helicopter. Wyatt followed on his own and
took her hand.

Maggie already knew that her Mom and the kids
were waiting at the house, preferring to have their
reunion in private, but Daddy stood next to his
pickup truck, squinting into the sunlight, the breeze
blowing his sandy hair over his brow.

Maggie wasn't up to running, but she hurried,
with Wyatt's help, and her father clutched her to
him. He smelled so beautiful, of worn denim and

clean cotton. Maggie breathed it in deeply and heard Daddy choke, then clear his throat with a cough. After a moment, he held her away from him and over his shoulder she saw Kirk Lynch standing next to a red Moped. His tie-dye, Grateful Dead t-shirt hung over his tan cargo shorts, and he wore a knit hat over his graying hair.

He stepped over to Gray's side, and Maggie saw he was holding a plastic cup, opaque with condensation.

"You're late, and you look like crap." He held out the cup. "Wyatt called and said you were asking for my lemonade."

TWENTY-SIX

FRIDAY, JULY 13TH 9:13 PM

The lawn surrounding the pool area was trimmed to perfection. The palm trees had beds of healthy flowers planted at their feet, and tastefully invisible solar lights played it all up to its carefully designed potential.

Gavin Betancourt, dressed in a white silk shirt and black trousers, kicked off his expensive Italian shoes and sat down at one of several patio tables, where a crystal tumbler held two fingers of aged bourbon.

The weather had gone from stormy to postcard-perfect balmy; the breeze off Tampa Bay was warm and silky, like a caress.

Gavin raised the glass to his lips, felt the smooth bourbon slide into his mouth. He held it there for a moment before he swallowed, enjoyed the warmth of it as it spread through his chest. He had just set the glass down when someone appeared at the edge of the light that surrounded the pool.

Gavin stood, thinking at first that it was one of his security people. But once he got a better look, he knew he didn't recognize the man who stood there with his arms at his sides, holding something long and thin in his right hand. It rested against the man's leg, almost reaching the ground. Gavin couldn't tell what it was, only that it wasn't a gun.

"Who are you?" Gavin asked sharply. Somebody on his security team was getting fired tonight.

The man reached up with his free hand and scratched gently at his eyebrow with one gloved hand before speaking, his voice smooth and calm.

"I'm Bennett Boudreaux."

Gavin took a step closer, squinted into the darkness that enveloped the stranger. After a few seconds, his eyes adjusted. Yes, he knew the man from numerous articles and TV stories, fundraisers and political rallies.

"What are you doing here?" he asked, his heart thumping just a bit harder.

"Don't be silly," Boudreaux said quietly.

"I didn't know," Gavin blurted. "I didn't know until my lawyer told me this morning."

"You didn't know what?

"Look…"

"You didn't know what?" Boudreaux repeated calmly.

"I didn't know she was your daughter!"

Boudreaux reached over and fiddled with the thing in his right hand. "Are you trying to say you didn't know her connection to me?"

Gavin swallowed as the man took a few steps closer, stopping just at the edge of the patio. Where was his security team?

"I knew—I thought she was your girlfriend," he said.

"Is that right?" Boudreaux tilted his head, like a curious cat, and a shaft of light from the patio reached across his face. His eyes were the weirdest shade of blue, and they looked right into Gavin.

"Yes," he said. "I didn't—"

"Why would you think that?"

"Bledsoe told me when he first got to Franklin County."

"I see," Boudreaux said. He raised the thing he was holding out in front of him, and Gavin saw, with a sinking sensation in his gut, that it was some kind of spear gun, like divers used.

"Please—" Gavin started.

"If I were you, I'd have words with Bledsoe next time you see him," Boudreaux said.

Gavin just had time to open his mouth before he heard a soft *thump* and something slammed into his chest.

$$\updownarrow \quad \updownarrow \quad \updownarrow$$

Wyatt dropped his toothbrush into the glass jar by the sink, and walked into the bedroom wearing his Crimson Tide pajama pants and an old t-shirt. He stopped and jammed his fists onto his hips.

Coco was draped across the entire width of the foot of the bed, where Wyatt's feet were supposed to go. Maggie was lying in the middle of the bed, the covers pulled up to her hips. Kyle was on the near side of her, Sky on the other.

Wyatt's gaze dropped to Maggie's chest.

"No," he said firmly.

Stoopid's stupid head was poking out from Maggie's collar. The rest of him was a lump underneath her pink t-shirt.

"What?" Maggie asked, like she couldn't imagine the answer. "He's been really stressed out. This is where he used to sleep when he was a chick."

"Yeah? Well, I've been really stressed out, too, and *I* was gonna sleep there."

"Ew," Sky sang. "The youth are present."

"Come on, Wyatt," Maggie said, laughing just a little. She still looked pale and tired; her lips were still chapped and her voice was still wonky, but she was coming along nicely.

"Move over, Kyle," Wyatt said.

Kyle scooted closer to his Mom, taking his pillow with him and propping it behind his head.

"We're not going to do this every night now, are we?" Wyatt asked with mock indignation.

"Chill, Wyatt Earp."

"Shut up, Sky."

Kyle picked the remote up from where it lay on the covers, then clicked on the flat-screen TV.

"You sure this is what you want to watch?" he asked his mom.

"Yes," she said, smiling.

"We've seen Lilo & Stitch like a hundred times."

"I don't care."

"Do we have to sing the songs, too?" Sky asked.

"Yes," she and Wyatt said in unison.

⚓   ⚓   ⚓

ONE WEEK LATER

Maggie sat on the cool sand, her arms wrapped around her knees.

The storms had gone, and calmer weather had come to St. George Island. The surf was light, and the sandpipers happily ran back and forth from the water. One white heron stood stoically at the water's edge, staring out at the water like he was waiting for a ferry.

Maggie had been given a clean bill of health and the okay to go back to work. Gavin Betancourt had been found near his swimming pool three days prior, and he was not given a clean bill of health at all.

Wyatt, as acting Sheriff, had looked immediately into Boudreaux's whereabouts at the time Betancourt and three security guards were killed, but Miss Evangeline, Amelia, and two employees of the seafood company gave him the same alibi. Wyatt declared he really didn't give a crap who killed Betancourt and pronounced it Tampa's problem.

Despite being cleared to work, Maggie had decided to take another week off.

She stood up and stretched her legs, causing the heron to flap its wings in irritation. She looked over her shoulder and across the sand.

Boudreaux stood on the second-story deck of one of his vacation rentals, his elbows resting on the rail and his hands clasped together. For a moment, Maggie wondered if he was praying. Then he smiled at her, and she smiled back before turning back to the water.

The water on the island was very shallow, not getting past four feet until about twenty feet off shore.

Maggie took a deep breath, tugged at the bottom of her one-piece bathing suit, and smiled nervously.

Then she ran for four good strides and dove in.

A NOTE

Have you missed any of the previous books in the Forgotten Coast Florida Suspense series? You can find them all right here. You might also enjoy my first novel, *See You.*

If you want to know when new books are released or about appearances and book signings, you can sign up for my newsletter or just follow my Facebook page. We have a lot of fun over there.

If you haven't yet started The Still Waters Suspense series, about Wyatt's friend, Evan Caldwell, you can check out the first two chapters of the first book in the series, *Dead Reckoning*, right now. It's set one county over from Apalach, in lovely Port St. Joe, FL, and is co-written with a good friend; the real Axel Blackwell. There's no rooster, but there is a really cool cat.

ONE

People who dream about quiet country nights have never been in the country after dark.

Even after their dogs had shut up, Mooney White and Grant Woodburn were surrounded by nothing but noise. The crickets and the frogs were screaming at each other, and there was a light breeze, nice for June, moving through the trees that had been bothersome to the men before they'd finally bagged their fill.

It was just past three in the morning, and dark-dark. The men were in the ass end of Gulf County, FL, in the woods just north of Wewahitchka and near the Dead Lakes Recreation Area. The low, thick cloud cover made the moon pointless.

Mooney was a black man in his late forties. He was dressed in an old pair of his blue work pants and a navy windbreaker. The many spots of white in his close-cropped hair looked like a little patch of fireflies in the night. He used his flashlight to guide their steps over rocks and fallen limbs. His .22 rifle was slung over his shoulder, and he held his dog's leash in the other hand.

Grant Woodburn, a redheaded man just a bit younger than his best friend, held his dog's leash in one hand, and a .410 single shot in the other. Their bag of coons was slung around his neck.

The men's boots crunched softly atop the thick carpet of pine needles. Ahead of them, the two dogs were almost soundless in their passage.

It was Mooney who first spotted the dim lights. They rounded a thick copse of shrubs and old cypress, and the two circles of light were just visible through the trees, about a hundred yards ahead.

"Hey, Woodburn," he said. "You left the lights on in my truck, I'm gonna kill you."

Woodburn stopped and looked at the lights. "Man, I didn't leave your lights on," he said. There was a high-pitched buzzing near his right ear, and he brushed at it with the sleeve of his Carhartt jacket. "We ain't even over there." He lifted his arm again and pointed off to the right. "We're over there."

Mooney's dog, a fawn-colored Ladner Black Mouth cur, went to tugging on his leash. Mooney tensed up on the leash and made a sound almost like he was getting something out of his teeth. The dog stopped, and the leash got some slack to it again. Mooney stopped, too.

"Those lights is about out," he said. "Somebody's gonna be pissed when they get back to their vehicle."

Woodburn looked over at him as he jerked slightly on his own leash. His brown and white Beagle stood stiffly where he was, looking toward the truck.

"Reckon we should go shut his lights off for him?" Woodburn asked.

"If the fool left his doors unlocked," Mooney answered.

"Man, this is right around where we heard that shot a while back," Woodburn said, his voice slightly hushed.

Mooney stopped walking. His dog and then his friend followed suit.

"That don't necessarily mean nothin'," Mooney said quietly.

"Maybe we should just go to your truck and call the police or somethin'," Woodburn whispered.

"Man, we got two guns," Mooney said. "Besides, what are we gonna tell 'em? Haul y'all asses out here to shut this fool's lights off? You watch too much TV."

He made a clicking noise with his tongue, and men and dogs veered off their intended path and headed for the lights. When they were about fifty feet out, Mooney squinted at the pickup that sat silently in the clearing. From where they STOOD they were looking at the truck head on. The driver's side door was standing open. The interior light either didn't work or had already burned out.

"I know that truck," Mooney said under his breath.

It was a black Ford F-150, which in Gulf County was like saying its name was John. But the Gators antenna topper was ringing a bell for Mooney.

"Whose is it?" Woodburn asked.

"Hold on, I'm thinking," Mooney answered. He was quiet for a moment. "That's Sheriff Hutchins' truck."

"Are you sure?" his friend asked him.

"Yeah, man, I put a new tranny in it last year," Mooney answered.

"Aw, man, I don't like it," Woodburn said. His beagle, Trot, had set to whining.

"I'm not real excited, either," Mooney said. "But maybe he needs help or somethin'."

"Not from us, man," Grant said. "Maybe from the cops."

"Man, pull your pants up," Mooney said. "Norman, let's go," he said to his dog, and started following him slowly into the clearing.

Mooney and Norman were in the lead, Woodburn and Trot lagging a bit behind, which was definitely Woodburn's choice and not the dog's. The beagle strained at his leash.

As Mooney got closer, he realized that the weird shininess on the driver's side window wasn't some trick of the light. Something on the window, all over it. He stopped walking. A thin sheet of moisture had suddenly appeared on his onyx skin, and he swiped at it with one huge, calloused hand.

"Sheriff?" he called out, flicking his flashlight on and off against the windshield. The flashlight wasn't a particularly powerful one. Its light bounced off the glass, revealing nothing. "Hey, Sheriff? It's Mooney White!"

The crickets and frogs went silent. For a few moments, there was just the wind in the trees and the quiet keening of the dogs.

"Shut up, Norman!" Mooney snapped, and both dogs quieted. A new sound, a faint one, reached Mooney's ears. "You hear that?"

Both men listened for a moment. "Radio," Woodburn whispered finally.

"Hell's up in here?" Mooney asked himself mostly.

He flicked the flashlight on again, trained it at the open door. In the edge of the light, he saw something, and dropped the beam lower. Beneath the door, he saw pants. Knees of pants. And one hand just hanging there.

"Aw hell, man," Woodburn whispered. "This ain't right at all."

Mooney slid his rifle down his arm, released the safety with his flashlight hand. The light bobbed off to the side of the truck.

"Sheriff?" Mooney called again. "Scarin' Mooney just a little bit here."

There was no answer. Norman gave out a couple of barks, higher-pitched than some people would expect from such a sturdy dog. Mooney gave him his lead, and followed Norman as the dog pulled toward the truck. Mooney tugged him off to the side, made him circle wide, about eight or ten feet from the old Ford. He could hear Woodburn several yards behind him, whispering to himself.

When Mooney had gotten round to the back side of the open door, he pointed the flashlight at it.

"Oh, hellfire," Mooney said to himself.

Sheriff Hutchins was slumped forward on his knees, his upper body hung up on the open door. Closer up, the black on the window wasn't black at all, but a deep red, and there was a lot more of it on the inside of the door.

Mooney stood there staring, barely hearing his best friend gagging behind him, or Lynyrd Skynrd on the Sheriff's truck radio, singing about going home.

TWO

The cell phone bleated, vibrated, and did a little jig on the built-in teak nightstand. Evan Caldwell reached over and thumbed the answer button without looking at the screen.

"This is Vi," a deep voice intoned before he had a chance to speak.

"So it would seem," Evan answered. She always said it like that, deliberately and with brevity, like a newscaster introducing himself.

"You need to get out to Wewa," she said. "It's very serious."

"I'm off today, Vi," he said.

"Not anymore," she said, her voice like gravel that had been soaked in lye. "We need you to get out there immediately."

"I don't think that I actually know where it is," he said.

"You may not know how to pronounce Wewahi-tchka, but certainly you can recognize it on a map," she replied. "Take 71 straight to Wewa. Go to the Shell station at the intersection of 71 and 22. You'll be met by Chief Beckett."

"Is he an Indian chief?"

He heard Vi try to sigh quietly. She was Sheriff Hutchins' assistant, and had apparently been with the Sheriff's Office since law enforcement was invented. Evan had only been there a few weeks and had yet to make a good impression on her. Granted, he hadn't put forth much effort. It seemed rather pointless, considering he was from "out of town" and would probably be gone again before she could decide if she liked him.

"He is the Chief of Police in Wewa," she said. "Lieutenant Caldwell, this is a very grave matter, which I don't want to explain over the phone. Chief Beckett will fill you in, then lead you to the scene."

Evan was mostly awake at this point, and her voice told him that his sarcasm would be unappreciated and possibly inappropriate.

"Did the Sheriff ask you to call me?" he asked her as he sat up.

There was silence on her end for a moment. When she finally spoke, he thought maybe her voice cracked just a little. "Please just go, as quickly as possible," she said, and hung up.

Evan looked at his phone for a moment, then checked the time. It was just after four in the morning. He swung his legs over the side of the bed and rubbed at his face as the teak sole of the master stateroom chilled his feet.

Evan was just shy of forty-two and starting to collect tiny lines at the corners of his eyes and crease lines along the sides of his mouth. His eyes were a bright, clear green that was surprising beneath his black hair and thick eyelashes. The very narrow, white scar that ran from the left corner of his mouth down to his chin kept him from being too pretty, or so his wife Hannah liked to say.

He stood up, took two steps over to the hanging locker beside his bed. One of the many reasons he'd chosen the 1986 Chris-Craft Corinthian over some of the other boats he'd seen was that it had a master stateroom with an actual bed and some halfway decent storage. Evan hadn't kept much when he'd emptied the Cocoa Beach house and moved aboard the boat, but he liked everything to have a place, and to be there when he expected it to be.

He opened the locker, pulled a pair of black trousers from their hanger and slipped them on. Three identical pairs remained in the locker, next to three identical navy trousers and five identical white button-down shirts. As he bent to step into his pants, he swore he could smell cat urine. His upper lip twitched as he leaned into the locker and sniffed. The only light in the room came from the lights on the dock, shining vague and gray through the curtains over the portholes.

His shoes, two pairs of black dress shoes, one pair of Docksiders, and a pair of running shoes, were lined up neatly on a shelf at the bottom of the locker. He bent lower, and the scent magnified. He picked up a shoe from the middle, a left dress shoe. The inside was shinier than it ought to be. He brought it to his nose and jerked back.

He managed to stop himself from throwing the shoe across the room, distributing cat pee throughout his cabin, but just barely. Instead, he carefully set it down on the floor, and pulled a shirt from the locker.

Once he had dressed, he walked in his sock feet into the boat's one head, which the previous owner had fortuitously remodeled just before he got divorced and had to sell. The guy had expanded it into the space that had been a closet, which gave him room to put in a real shower, and a space for a stacking washer and dryer. It only fit the type that people used in RVs, but it was enough for Evan, who had trouble using public appliances and would prefer buying new clothes every week to going to a laundromat.

Evan grabbed his cleaning tote from the top of the small dryer, wet a cloth with a mixture of warm water and the expensive wood soap, stalked back to the hanging locker, and thoroughly cleaned and dried the small, sloped shelf on which he kept his shoes. Then he carried the wet shoe up to the galley, tied it up in a trash bag, and set the trash bag just outside the French door to the large sun deck.

When he came back inside, he spotted the cat sitting on the built-in teak cabinet between the steps down to the V-berth Evan used for storage and the steps down to the galley. Plutes was as black as ebony and weighed at least fifteen pounds. Hannah had brought him home just a few weeks before Evan's life had fallen apart, and said she'd named him Pluto. Plutes for short.

Evan had thought she'd named him after the idiot dog from Disney. In fact, she'd taken the name from a Poe story. Evan didn't read Poe's stories, although he liked The Raven quite a bit, so he could never remember which story it was, but he thought the name was probably appropriate anyway.

The cat had never made a sound in all the time Evan had been burdened with him; at least none that Evan had been there to hear. He was a shiny, black statue of seething disdain and discontent. He turned away from one of the windows that wrapped around the entire salon and stared at Evan over his shoulder, his eyes narrowed and dismissive.

"Was that you?" Evan asked the cat, then cringed at the realization that he had become one of those people who asked cats questions. It was also a stupid question, since Plutes was the only cat aboard.

Plutes blinked at Evan, just once, slowly. Then he looked back out the window. If he could sigh, he clearly would have.

"Do it again and you'll go to the pound," Evan said, then went down the three steps that led to the eat-in galley. It was small but got good light from the windows in the salon, and it suited Evan's needs. To one side was the U-shaped galley itself, with fairly new stainless appliances and two feet of gray Corian countertop that was just enough. On the other side, a built-in dinette booth with blue striped upholstery and a small window.

Evan poured a cup of milk two thirds full and set it in the microwave to heat, then loaded up his espresso machine and turned it on. Vi had sounded distressed, and no doubt the call was urgent, but Evan had only had three hours of sleep. He wouldn't get to We-whatever any faster by crashing.

While the espresso brewed, Evan walked back to his stateroom and retrieved the undefiled dress shoes from the locker. He slipped these on, then opened a side table drawer, and pulled out his holster, his badge and his Sheriff's Office ID. He dropped the ID wallet into his pocket, clipped the holster over his belt on the right side, and fastened his badge to the front of his belt on the left.

There was a decent breeze coming through the open windows, and the air smelled briny and clean simultaneously. Evan took a deep lungful of it and mourned the day out on the water that he'd had planned. Then he went back to the galley, poured the milk and espresso into his travel mug, and took three swallows before he headed back up to the salon.

He returned Plutes' look of disgust as he crossed the salon, then stepped out onto the sun deck. It was Evan's favorite part of the boat, large enough for a rattan table and chairs and a decent stainless BBQ. He picked up the trash bag containing the stinking shoe and walked it out to a garbage can on the dock. Then he headed down the long dock toward the main marina building, now mostly dark, and the lights of Port St. Joe, FL. It was mostly dark, too.

Aside from the creaking of fenders against the dock and the clinking of mast rigging on the few sailboats nearby, the sound of Evan's footfalls was the only noise that disturbed the infant morning.

A NOTE FROM THE AUTHOR

Thank you for spending some time with these characters, and this place, that I love so much.

If you'd like to be the first to know about the next book in the series, other new releases, or events and appearances, please sign up for my newsletter, *UnForgotten*, at

DAWNLEEMCKENNA.COM

You can also hang out with myself and other readers on the Dawn Lee McKenna Facebook page. We have a lot of fun over there.

If you've missed any of the books in this series, my first book, See You, or the books in the new spin-off series about Wyatt's friend Evan Caldwell, you can find them right here:

WWW.AMAZON.COM/GP/PRODUCT/B07CTNPZ3S

Many thanks, as always, to my wonderful editor, Debbie Maxwell Allen, my book designer, Colleen

Sheehan of Ampersand Book Interiors, and my cover designer, the amazing Shayne Rutherford of Wicked Good Book Covers.

Thank you, too, to everyone at Sweet Tea Publishing: CFO Linda Maxwell, VP of Marketing Katherine Scheideler, Director of Florida Distribution and Appearances Chrystal Hartigan, and Director of Social Media and Relations Chelsey Reeves.

I'd like to thank all of the real people in who, generously and with good humor, have allowed me to turn them into fictional characters. Many thanks to John Solomon, Linda Joseph, Kirk and Faith Lynch, my good friend and co-writer Axel Blackwell, Apalach PD officer Chase Richards (otherwise known as Richard Chase), and Officer Shawn Chisolm, as well as to Mayor Van Johnson, Sheriff AJ Smith, the Apalachicola Police Department, and the Franklin County Sheriff's Office. All of you make these books something I could not make them on my own.

As always, so much gratitude to God, to my family, and to my friends, who put up with me so that I can write, and last but not least, to the most amazing readers any writer could hope to find. I love you all.

Made in USA - North Chelmsford, MA
1057121_9780998666952
03.19.2020 2057